RHINO CHARGE

VICTORIA TAIT

KANGA
PRESS

DEDICATION

For Andrew, William & Archie
Who supported me during these difficult times

GET EXCLUSIVE MATERIAL
BY JOINING MY BOOK CLUB

If you'd like to hear from me about my books, author life, new releases and special offers, then please join my book club. I don't send spam and you can unsubscribe at any time.

Building a relationship with my readers is one of the most exciting elements of being an author.

If you would like to receive regular updates, please visit VictoriaTait.com.

Thank you, and enjoy Rhino Charge.

KISWAHILI WORD GLOSSARY

- *Amref* Kenyan medics and flying doctor service
- *Asante* Thank you
- *Boda Boda* Motorbike used as a taxi
- *Bonnet* English word for the metal hood covering the car's engine
- *Bwana* Sir, a term of respect used for an older man
- *Habari* Greeting used like hello but meaning 'What news?'
- *Hapana* No
- *Jumper* Sweater/pullover
- *Kahawa* Coffee
- *Kanga* Colourful cotton fabric (also Swahili for guinea fowl)
- *Kikoi* Brightly coloured cotton garment or sarong
- *Kikuyu* Kenyan ethnic group or tribe
- *KWS* Kenyan Wildlife Service
- *Memsahib* A white foreign woman of higher status
- *Mitumba* Second-hand clothes, shoes and fabric market. Literal meaning is 'bundles' derived from

the plastic wrapped packages the donated clothing arrives in

- *Mundi Mugo* Kikuyu traditional medicine man
- *Mzungu* European/White person
- *Nagi* Kikuyu Supreme God
- *Namaste* Hindu greeting
- *Nyama Choma* Grilled/BBQ meat
- *Oryx* Large antelope
- *Pole* Sorry
- *Samosa* Fried pastry with savoury filling
- *Sawa (sawa)* Fine, all good, no worries.
- *Shuka* Thin, brightly coloured blanket in bright checked colours, where red is often the dominant colour. Also used as a sarong or throw
- *Tusker & Whitecap* Brands of beer brewed by East African Breweries
- "Yagna shishta shinah shanto muchyante sarva kil bishaihi. Bhunjya tete tvagham papa, ye pachantyatma karnat." Hindu prayer said before a meal which means: A righteous person who eat the food after offered for sacrifice are released from all sins. The others who cook and eat solely for their own sake, eat sin.

STYLE, SPELLING AND PHRASEOLOGY

Mama Rose, the main character through whose eyes we view events, has a British education and background. She uses British phrases, spelling and style of words.

Kiswahili words are also used in the book so there is a Glossary at the front, which briefly explains their meaning.

These words add to the richness and authenticity of the setting and characters, and I hope increase your enjoyment of Rhino Charge.

THE RHINO CHARGE

The Rhino Charge is a unique off-road event, and whilst it may seem a strange subject for a cozy mystery, it is one of the highlights of Kenya's sporting and social calendar. It brings together Kenya's African, Indian, and European communities, annually raises large amounts of money for a conservation charity, and team places are highly sought after. I hope you enjoy the experience.

Officials

- Christian Lambrechts - Executive Director of Rhino Ark Charitable Trust
- Nick West - Chairman of the Rhino Charge Committee
- Tanya West
- Frank Butler
- Wendy Butler
- 'Mama Rose' Hardie
- Chloe Collins

Team/Car 27 Bandit Bush Hogs (Team Colours - Blue and Yellow)

- Kumar Chauhan - Manager
- Mayur Chauhan - Driver
- Jono Urquhart - Navigator
- Thabiti Onyango - Mechanic
- Sam Mwamba - Winchman
- George - Runner
- Marina Thakker - Runner

Team/Car 63 Rhino Force (Team Colours – Black)

- Deepak Seth - Driver & Manager
- Suvas Patel - Navigator
- Ricky Singh - Mechanic
- Hinesh Seth - Runner
- Aatma Seth - Runner
- Vijay Thakker - Runner

CHAPTER ONE

Rose squashed her clothes into her brown canvas bag and forced the zip closed.

"All packed," she exclaimed to her husband Craig, who was propped up in bed. Rose Hardie, fondly known as 'Mama Rose' by the local community, was a tall, thin, sprightly woman despite being sixty-five years old.

Her husband Craig, who was in his early seventies, was almost bed-bound. He had caught polio as a child and now a secondary complication was paralysing the left side of his body. Recently, he'd also suffered a mini-stroke.

"Now you're sure you'll be OK?" Rose asked. "I shall be away nearly a week."

"Stop fussing, woman. You've left me plenty of times before and I've survived." Craig's jaw set into a thin line. She had spent time away in the past, but that was before he had fallen ill.

Craig continued, "I have Kipto to look after me, and she'll make sure Samwell helps me out onto the patio for fresh air, or into the living room so I can watch horse racing from South Africa."

At the sound of her name, Kipto, their house girl of

unknown age, entered, closely followed by a fluffy white dog which resembled a small sheep.

Kipto turned to the dog and flapped her arms. "Shoo. Is this dog always hungry?" she asked. "It not stop following me."

"Its owner, Thabiti, is the hungry one," responded Rose. "I think she's scared of being alone again. She was abandoned in a locked house before Dr Emma rescued her." Pixel, the dog, jumped onto the bed and started sniffing Rose's bag. Potto, Rose's black and tan terrier, growled as it lay beside Craig's feet.

"I'm ready." She walked around the bed and pecked Craig on the top of his balding head. "It won't be the same at the Rhino Charge this year without you. Do you know, we've never missed a Charge since it started in 1989." Rose looked down as Craig smiled weakly at her. They both knew he was unlikely to attend another.

"Just keep out of trouble," Craig told her.

Rose parked her battered, red Land Rover Defender in a free space beside Mr Obado's garage in the centre of Nanyuki, a small market town, three hours' drive north of Nairobi, the capital of Kenya. A crowd of people gathered outside the garage and watched a blue 4x4 car being loaded onto a long flat-bed trailer. The vehicle started life as a Range Rover, but it had been stripped down to its skeleton and rebuilt into a robust off-road machine capable of travelling across rough terrain.

Rose stood next to a young African man with cropped hair and a neat beard and moustache.

"Thabiti, am I OK on your side?" the driver shouted as he drove onto the trailer's ramp.

"Plenty of room," the young man called back.

A well-dressed, attractive blonde-haired lady joined them. "Morning, Chloe," Rose greeted the new arrival.

Chloe pressed her hands together and exclaimed, "So this is the car you've been hiding. It's a beast."

Thabiti grinned. "This event is not called the Rhino Charge for nothing. The vehicles have to be strong enough to navigate sandy slopes, rocky ground, and force their way through bushes, just as a real Rhino would."

Chloe slipped on a large pair of sunglasses. "I've never really understood the fascination between men and cars, but I am looking forward to spending a week in the Maasai Mara. I can't wait to see all the wildlife."

Rose turned to her and said, "We'll be working, so I'm not sure how much time we'll get for safaris."

Chloe's mouth drooped.

At that moment Rose's mobile phone rang. The voice on the other end said, "Hi, Rose. Are you busy?"

Rose's heart sank. The caller was Dr Emma, who was technically her boss. Rose called herself a community vet, but when the Kenyan authorities altered the veterinary regulations, she became a veterinary paraprofessional, working under the only qualified vet in Nanyuki, Dr Emma. "Why? What's happened?"

"I've had a call from Ol Pejeta Conservancy. Ringo, the orphan rhino, is unwell."

"Just a minute," Rose said into the phone. She lifted her head. "Dr Emma needs my help at Ol Pejeta."

"But we'll miss our lift," cried Chloe.

"You go. I'll see if I can find someone else travelling to the Mara."

Chloe shook her head. "I'm not going alone."

CHAPTER TWO

R ose steered her trusty Defender around another large
pothole in the dirt track. Chloe and Dr Emma were
squeezed together in the passenger seats beside her. Dr
Emma was a diminutive figure, but she had a huge afro
hairstyle and wore enormous, round, yellow-rimmed
glasses.

"Why don't they mend this road?" Chloe wondered aloud.
"I'm surprised it's in such poor condition considering the
number of tourists who visit Ol Pejeta."

They arrived at the conservancy entrance and, after
signing the visitor's book, were ushered through.

"It's so green after the recent rains," pronounced Dr
Emma.

"Look, impala," cried Chloe.

Rose's two passengers bobbed up and down like excited
school children. Sweeping plains opened out ahead of them,
interspersed with denser areas of bushes and solitary acacia
trees.

"This is fantastic." Dr Emma gazed out through the
windscreen. "I don't get to visit Ol Pejeta very often. I just
don't seem to have the time."

Rose turned off the track beside Morani's Restaurant and parked outside the Rhino caretakers' wooden hut.

A serious-looking African man wearing green trousers, shirt, and matching short-brimmed hat strode to meet them with his arm outstretched. "Habari. I'm Zachariah." He shook hands with each of them. "Follow me."

They entered a large wooden enclosure with a dirt floor. At the far end stood a tiny dejected rhino, with a drooping head and ears pinned back against his stocky neck.

This was Ringo, who had been abandoned by his mother when he was only two weeks old. The team at Ol Pejeta had done a wonderful job nursing him back to health from his severely malnourished state. At an outreach day for the Giant's Club Summit, earlier in April, he had been the star attraction.

"He's so sweet," cried Chloe. "Why's he called Ringo?"

Zachariah answered, "After the famous musician who raises money for wildlife conservation, and has spoken out against rhino poaching. I think his band was called The Bugs."

Chloe wrinkled the corner of her mouth but Rose laughed. "I think he means Ringo Starr from The Beatles."

Chloe jumped as they heard a grunting noise and something hit the wooden partition against which she leant.

"It's OK, Sudan," soothed Zachariah. An enormous rhino on the far side of the fence stamped a foot. "He's really taken to Ringo. We were worried about his health as he's getting old, until this little one arrived and he perked up."

"What are you feeding Ringo?" asked Dr Emma.

Zachariah replied, "A mixture of lactose, porridge oats, glucose and salt. We usually feed him five or six times a day, but he won't touch it now."

"What about his usual routine?"

"Normally he is bright and loves his daily runs with one

of the caretakers. He's less keen on his mud-wallowing lessons, but now he refuses to leave this enclosure."

Rose said, "It's notoriously difficult raising young rhino. Is someone always with him?"

"Yes, and one of us always sleeps next to him at night."

Rose nodded. "Even so, it's not the same as having a mother. However hard you try, you can't replicate the care or education she should be giving him." She laid a hand on Zachariah's arm. "We'll do our best for him."

Rose knelt beside the small rhino. She ran her fingers gently across his thick hide, but couldn't find any cuts, or anything caught in or sticking out of it. She placed a hand on his shoulder. "He doesn't feel too hot. Actually, I think we should put a blanket on him."

Zachariah placed a red and blue checked shuka over Ringo's small frame.

"Keep trying him with water. We don't want him getting dehydrated," directed Dr Emma. "If he still refuses to eat his normal food, try some milk formula. And if he continues like this, and there is no obvious cause, we will need to test his blood to see if he is fighting a virus, or lacking any vitamins or minerals."

Rose, Chloe and Dr Emma were subdued as they left the conservancy, and took little notice of the warthogs, rushing away from the noise of the car, with erect tails.

CHAPTER THREE

The next day was Friday. Rose and Craig were enjoying breakfast at their outdoor dining table on their cottage's covered patio.

"Nick West sent me a text," said Rose. "Jono Urquhart, a pilot with Equator Air, is collecting provisions from Nanyuki tomorrow and flying back to the Rhino Charge with Nick's wife Tanya. He can give Chloe and me a lift."

"That'll be much better than an eight-hour drive. Jono Urquhart, he's Kenyan isn't he? I'm sure there were Urquharts living in Lavington in Nairobi."

"I've no idea, but I am grateful for the offer."

Craig buttered his toast. "I also received a text, from Thabiti. He's arrived safely and inquired about Pixel. He asked if you have time to visit his sister in the Cottage Hospital."

Pearl, Thabiti's older sister, was not physically ill, but after the traumatic events surrounding her mother's death she had stopped eating, become very weak, and was suffering with mental health issues.

Rose dolloped yoghurt onto her fruit and muesli. "That works well. I've agreed with Dr Farrukh to drive you to the hospital for your appointment today. Her husband's been called away to Timau, so she's covering his morning clinic and cannot conduct her scheduled home visit."

❀

Craig and Rose sat patiently on padded plastic chairs in the waiting area of the Cottage Hospital's new administrative block. Rose wrinkled her nose, which was overpowered by a strong smell of disinfectant from the recently washed floor.

They watched an elderly African man being led though the entrance. Although he walked slowly, his back was straight and proud. But his eyes had the milkiness of a blind man. He was assisted to a chair outside the registrar's office.

Rose turned to Craig. "Isn't that Mr Kariuki?"

"I haven't seen him for years," replied Craig. "I didn't realise he'd lost his sight. I'm sure the last time I saw him he was still a practicing psychologist."

"I wonder if he can help Pearl? I heard that his approach of combining the craft of a traditional Kikuyu medicine man with modern psychology works wonders for a troubled soul."

Rose approached the old man. "Habari, Bwano."

Mr Kariuki clapped his hands together. "Mama Rose, how wonderful, but you don't sound ill." His voice steadied. "Is it Craig?"

"I'm afraid so. He's had some health issues and we're here for a check-up."

"Mama, you cannot deceive me. I am a dying man and I recognise from your voice that Craig may be, too." She had forgotten how perceptive Mr Kariuki was. "Make sure his last precious days are overflowing with joy and wonder. You've always known how to live a full life."

She was relieved the old man couldn't see her blush as

she asked, "Have you come across a young woman called Pearl in the hospital?"

"Ah yes, she has a troubled heart, but it will not heal while she remains inside her own head."

"If you see her again, can you speak to her? Her mother, a childhood friend of mine, died recently. I think she was rather over-protective and controlling when it came to Pearl. And Pearl's current state has been made worse by choosing a man who, well, let's say he treated her badly."

"There is much you are withholding, but I will look out for the young woman, although she may not wish to speak to a blind old man."

"Craig Hardie," a nurse called.

Rose returned to Craig and helped him into Dr Farrukh's consulting room.

CHAPTER FOUR

R ose's stomach lurched as she was thrust against her restraining seat belt. Chloe screamed as tree tops rose rapidly to meet them. Suddenly, the forest vanished and they were thrown back into their places as the six-seater Cessna plane levelled off and they soared out over the vast expanse of Kenya's Great Rift Valley.

"Sorry, ladies. We caught a downdraft as we flew over the edge of the Aberdare Mountain range. It's always the trickiest part of the flight," announced their jaunty pilot.

Rose fell back against the headrest in relief. She had been born and brought up in rural Kenya and was well aware of the perils of its third largest mountain range. Despite the dangers, it was the route most planes flew between Nairobi and northern Kenya, including Nanyuki, where she lived. She looked down and wondered if she spotted the outline of a plane wing. The mountains had claimed many lives and not all the bodies had been recovered.

Rose glanced towards her younger companion. Chloe's suntanned face was pale and her neat, manicured hands gripped the seat rests. Rose was not sure of Chloe's precise age, but thought she was in her mid- to late-thirties. Chloe's husband Dan had left the British Army and taken a job with a security firm in Kenya.

They had only arrived in Nanyuki a few months earlier, but Dan already spent most of his time away with work. Chloe tried to keep herself busy and had jumped at the chance to take Craig's place as an official at the Rhino Charge.

A woman's voice sounded through Rose's headphones. "That was exciting," she shrilled. "Are you all right back there?" Although Tanya West was only in her late-twenties, her voice took on a bossy tone. "You are lucky Jono was flying to collect me, and my husband suggested he offer you a lift after you missed yours."

The colour returned to Chloe's face and she turned to Rose with flushed cheeks and large questioning eyes.

Rose shook her head and said, "Thank you, Jono. Yes very fortunate, my dear, but your husband relies on volunteers like us. He wouldn't be able to afford the cost of running the Rhino Charge if he had to pay for helpers. Besides, we are all doing this to raise money for a wildlife charity."

Rose heard a deep intake of breath over the headphones. She spotted Chloe clamp a hand over her mouth as her shoulders began to shake.

"Ladies, if you look down you'll see Lake Naivasha," instructed their pilot. Jono Urquhart must be in his late thirties, Rose thought. He had unruly ginger hair, a bushy beard and a relaxed, genial manner.

The Rift Valley spread before them with tarmac roads and brown dirt tracks criss-crossing it like strands of a spider's web. She looked down on several neat plots, each consisting of a tin-roofed house with a small field, enclosed by a wooden fence or trees.

She said, "I can hardly believe this area was so influential in our evolution. I understand our ancestors roamed here three million years ago, and it's where they developed the ability to walk upright."

"There's much debate about that," Tanya retorted.

"Never mind walking, ladies. The focus of the next few days is driving. Prepare yourselves to touch down at the official Mara landing strip for the 2016 Rhino Charge."

As the small plane began its descent, Rose was able to pick out groups of antelope grazing peacefully, and in the distance, three long-necked giraffes turned to contemplate them. She braced herself as the plane bumped and jumped onto the dusty runway and decelerated rapidly, throwing Rose once more into the back of her seat.

As the rotor spun to a stop, Jono jumped out and walked around the plane. He helped Rose down as she blinked in the bright sunlight. Chloe followed, wearing her sunglasses. The air was dry and full of dust from the landing.

"The rains came early to the Mara, but they've been absent now for several weeks. So it should be dry for this year's Rhino Charge," Jono told them.

A blue-clad African man ran towards them from a Land Cruiser car. He waved the keys at Jono, who shook his head.

"A pilot that doesn't like driving," observed Chloe.

"Something like that." Jono averted his gaze. He opened a locker on the outside of the plane. "Let's unload your luggage and be on our way."

They removed their bags and bedrolls: thin mattresses and bedding wrapped in waterproof canvas sacks which were rolled up for travelling. They also unloaded Chloe's cool box, fresh fruit and vegetables, first aid supplies and drinking water.

Jono grabbed a brown cardboard tube. "I mustn't forget this. It is our final sponsor's banner to stick onto the side of our car."

"You're competing?" Chloe gasped.

"Of course. I'm in the same team as Thabiti. He's the mechanic and I'm the navigator. Unfortunately, our main sponsor and driver injured his foot playing hockey and is hobbling around on crutches. His son is stepping in." Jono wrinkled his nose. "Right, that's it. Let's go."

CHAPTER FIVE

T he car crested the summit of a small hill and the Rhino Charge Headquarters appeared before them. It consisted of a central area of large and medium-sized white pointed tents surrounded by individual camps, each with a cluster of smaller tents.

Tanya informed them, "Ladies, you will be staying in the officials' camp at the far end where it's quietest. The spectators can be a rowdy bunch, so they're contained in an area next to the entrance. The teams set up their camps in between."

The car stopped behind a line of 4x4s queuing at the entrance, where vertical banners announced the 27th Annual Rhino Charge.

"Wow, look at all that kit," exclaimed Chloe. Each car was festooned with spare fuel cans, tyres, large water canisters, bags, and camping equipment.

"You can only use what you carry out here," explained Jono.

"Where are our passes?" demanded Tanya. Their driver reached into the glovebox and extracted a brown envelope. Tanya tipped the contents onto her lap. "Yellow bracelets this year for officials." She handed Chloe and Rose each a yellow vinyl strip with holes at one end and a plastic click lock at the other.

Chloe assisted Rose.

"Not too tight!" Rose exclaimed.

Chloe snapped Rose's bracelet into place. "Do competitors have a different colour?"

Jono held up his wrist. "Green for us and blue for our supporters."

"Red for the spectators, so we can quickly spot if they are in the wrong place," stated Tanya.

They passed through the entrance with their arms raised to show their bracelets, and parked in front of a large tent at the centre of the headquarters.

"Ladies, jump out and we'll drop your kit at your tent," Jono directed.

"Welcome," a voice cried, and they turned towards a fraught-looking man wearing shorts, with sunglasses balanced on his head of fair hair. He wiped his eyes before pecking Tanya on the cheek. "I'm so pleased you're here, darling." He turned to Rose with outstretched arms. "And you, Rose. And this must be Chloe." Chloe reached out and he shook her hand. "Registration opens in twenty minutes, so it's full on. Are you able to help?"

Chloe and Rose nodded.

"Great. Go grab yourselves a coffee. Open a tab with the Rusty Nail caterers and we'll settle up at the end of the event. We all have a food and drink allowance."

"Fetch me a white coffee, no sugar," called Tanya before entering an open-fronted tent. Two men were securing a banner above the entrance proclaiming 'Registration'.

Chloe rolled her eyes.

Rose turned and looked around. To the left was a line of

white pointed tents and opposite was the food and catering area. Cars and people milled about everywhere.

"Is it always this chaotic?" asked Chloe.

"Yes, but it used to be much smaller," mused Rose. "Craig and I were involved with the first event in 1989, when thirty-one cars took part. Now there are over sixty, with huge team entourages. Actually, they've limited the number of spectators as too many were coming from Nairobi for a party. You know, back in the first year, we were delighted to raise 250,000 Kenyan shillings, but now the Charge raises over 100 million shillings. That's a lot more pressure on the organisers. You just met Nick West, Tanya's husband. He is the one who runs the event."

"Are you missing Craig?" Chloe asked.

"Yes. It was because of him we were asked to get involved when it started. I prefer horses to cars, but officiating at the Rhino Charge has become an annual fixture. But it'll not be the same without him."

CHAPTER SIX

"There's a Dorman's Coffee trailer," Chloe pointed. "Let me buy you a tea. And I need a proper cappuccino."

"Now don't forget Tanya's coffee," Rose said. They joined a small queue.

Chloe lifted her sunglasses and secured them in her long blonde hair. "Can you explain again how the Rhino Charge works?"

They shuffled forward as the queue moved. Rose began, "Each team is made up of two to six people and a 4x4 car, which has to be registered to drive on Kenyan roads."

Reaching the front of the queue, Chloe ordered their drinks. Rose continued, "The teams are required to visit thirteen checkpoints scattered over one hundred kilometres of rough terrain. The competitors have ten hours to complete the task and the winner is the car which reaches all the check points, and travels the shortest distance."

Rose took her tea from Chloe, added milk and swirled the tea bag around before discarding it in a rubbish bin. Chloe picked up the coffees and frowned. "So the winner is not the quickest team to reach all the checkpoints."

"Exactly," agreed Rose. "The teams have to think about

their route and the terrain. Just wait, you'll be amazed at how they battle across uneven and rocky ground, push through dense thickets and even winch their cars up and down rocky outcrops."

Rose put her arm out to prevent Chloe being knocked over by Team 1 in a bright yellow 4x4, stripped of all comforts and fitted with oversized wheels. Company names were haphazardly stuck across it.

Chloe asked, "So what's the point?"

Rose laughed. "There is no point. A bunch of crazy mzungus and Indians, and now some equally barmy Kenyans, spend a fortune on vehicles which are too impractical to travel far in for any distance. Then they try their best to damage their cars by attempting insane manoeuvres, in the middle of nowhere, and it's all in the name of charity. Afterwards, the teams mend and improve their vehicles and it's a race to enter the following year's competition."

They stepped into a small tent beside the one for registration. Hard-backed posters hung along the sides of the tent and leaflets were strewn across a table.

Rose picked one up. "The beneficiary is the Rhino Ark Charitable Trust. It began by fencing the Aberdare National Park, over which we flew, to reduce poaching. Now the Trust is enclosing the Eburu Forest, as it suffers from illegal logging and charcoal burning. It's also involved with projects on Mount Kenya, building fences in the most densely populated areas, as these are where there is the most conflict between the wildlife and people."

"So what is our role?" asked Chloe.

"On Monday, the day of the Charge, we'll man a guard post which is one of the thirteen checkpoints. Now we need to help register the teams."

CHAPTER SEVEN

Team 27 called themselves the Bandit Bush Hogs and their team colours were bright blue and yellow. They had established their camp behind the registration tent in an open area of red oat grass.

Two clusters of tents, to the left and right, were positioned under the shade of thorny, flat-topped desert date trees. In the centre was a cream-coloured, domed, canvas events shelter, with blue-coloured trimmings and open sides. The Bandit Bush Hogs used it as their mess tent where they gathered for meals and team meetings.

The head of the team, Kumar Chauhan, often relaxed in the shelter and was joined by his daughter-in-law, Lavanya, and sometimes by his eldest son, Mayur. Two other team members, Jono Urquhart and Thabiti Onyango also used the shelter.

To the right, in a clear, sandy area, with no red oat grass, a large round metal fire pit had been positioned. Near it was a pile of branches and twigs gathered by the African camp staff.

A larger desert date tree rose behind the events shelter, providing additional shade for it and the cooking tent, which was hidden from the main camp by the trunk of the tree and a clump of thorny bushes.

The entrance to the Bandit Bush Hogs' camp was separated from the main camp by a line of camphor bushes, known locally as leleshwa bushes.

Thabiti Onyango was hidden under his team's bright blue 4x4 vehicle, which he had accompanied on its journey from Nanyuki on a flatbed trailer. He was only twenty and his mechanical experience was limited, but he'd learnt a lot working on the car at Mr Obado's garage.

He pushed at the undercarriage, making sure it was secure, and ran through different repair options in his head. It was quite likely the car would drive over, or land on, a sharp rock, which would damage a drive shaft or rip open one of the protective panels. He heard raised voices approach the car.

"Registration closes in fifteen minutes. We need to find that cheque, Jono, or we won't reach our entry fee pledge. Run through the places you might have left it," said an elderly male Indian voice. Thabiti recognised it as Kumar Chauhan, their team manager and former driver.

He liked Mr Chauhan better than Mayur, the team's new driver, who was arrogant and liked to throw his weight around. Whenever he got the opportunity he'd announce loudly, "We should have a qualified mechanic like the Rhino Force team." Just because they'd flown one in specially from the UK.

Thabiti smiled. Still, he was grateful Jono had suggested him as the team's mechanic and he was thankful Mr Chauhan had agreed. Few young Africans were given the opportunity to participate in such an exciting event. He just hoped it wouldn't be too difficult or dangerous. He twisted his head in the dirt and spotted the ends of Mr Chauhan's crutches.

Thabiti heard Jono say, "I landed at Equator Air and was driven into Nanyuki. At the Ford dealership the manager showed me the cheque before he placed it in a white envelope. But now I don't know where I put it."

"I hope you haven't left it on the plane. Let's check the car which picked you up."

As their voices retreated, Thabiti rolled out from under the car. He remembered the brown tube which contained the sponsor's poster. Jono said they'd fix it in place later, but he had time to do it now. He opened the tube, tipped out the contents, and unrolled a bright blue banner with the car dealer's name and logo. There was also a white envelope.

Thabiti turned towards Mr Chauhan and Jono and shouted, "Is this what you're looking for?" He waved the envelope in the air.

The men strode over and Mr Chauhan beamed. "Well done, Thabiti. Where did you find it?"

"Rolled up inside the sponsor's poster." Thabiti looked across at Jono.

"Of course, I must have dropped it into the tube. Thank you."

Thabiti caught sight of Jono's face tightening and his lips pressed together. But then he smiled and said, "For ensuring the Bandit Bush Hogs compete, you can hand the cheque over at registration."

A thin, attractive Indian lady wearing a long sleeve t-shirt and sari ran across. "You must hurry up. Mayur will be furious if you miss registration. Let me help you, Kumar."

The sleeve of her t-shirt wrinkled up as she offered her arm to Kumar, revealing a raw pink mark with blisters.

Kumar's brow furrowed and he asked, "Have you hurt yourself my dear?"

Hastily, she pulled her t-shirt down with her free hand. "It's nothing, just a burn. It's not easy cooking with charcoal safari ovens." She met Jono's gaze, but quickly averted her eyes.

"Jono, I think we should hurry." Thabiti twisted the envelope in his hand. "I'm sure Mr Chauhan will be OK following with Lavanya."

Jono blinked and said gruffly, "Of course. Come on."

CHAPTER EIGHT

At five o'clock, registration closed. Chloe stretched her hands up in the air. She had handed out safety equipment to all the teams which included a medical kit, red bag, emergency flags, and numbers for each car.

"Thabiti told me his camp is behind this tent. Can we visit him?" asked Chloe.

Rose replied, "OK, but we mustn't be too long as we need to organise our sleeping arrangements before it gets dark. Also, I'll need to find the nearest loo in case I get caught short in the night." Some aspects of growing old were challenging and she knew it was best to plan ahead.

They found a gap between the leleshwa bushes, with their waxy dark-green leaves and fluffy cotton-wool-like seed heads, and made their way across to the events shelter. Smoke floated up behind thorny bushes signalling that an evening meal was being cooked by camp staff.

Rose approached Kumar Chauhan. "Namaste," she greeted him and bowed her head. "I'm sorry to see you are injured and cannot compete for the Rhino Charge title."

Kumar Chauhan began to stand, but Rose put out a hand. "Please do not get up on my account Mr Chauhan."

"Mama Rose, you know you should call me Kumar. Is Craig with you?"

"Unfortunately, he's not well and has to miss this year's event."

"I am sorry to hear that. Please pass on my regards. Will you join us for a drink?"

Rose looked along the table. An attractive Indian woman, who had assisted Kumar in the registration tent a short time earlier, was placing cutlery on a blue-spotted PVC tablecloth. Jono watched her as he twirled a penknife between his fingers. At the other side of the table a middle-aged Indian man sat in a white plastic chair and opened a bottle of Tusker beer.

Rose replied, "Thank you, but Chloe and I only came to check on Thabiti and then we must return to our own camp. Another day perhaps." The two elderly people bowed their heads.

As Rose backed away, the middle-aged man announced, "Father, we really need some time to discuss my plans for the business before we get too busy with the Charge. I met some investors last week."

Kumar tapped his fingers on the table and replied, "We're away from Nairobi for the weekend to have fun and not talk business. Anyway, whilst I am still head of the company, we are not wasting money and moving to a fancy, new, expensive warehouse in Runda. The current one on Victory Estate is quite sufficient and convenient for our workers."

"But we need to expand."

"Mayur, that's enough. In the future, please don't go behind my back and talk to other people about our business."

Rose and Chloe sat down in folding metal-legged camp chairs next to Thabiti, by the unlit metal fire pit. Beside him was Marina, a young Indian woman, who Rose had met earlier in the month. She'd helped Chloe at the registration desk for the Laikipia Conservation Society's conference outside Nanyuki.

"Ow!" Chloe cried as she spotted Marina's face. "What happened to you?" The area around Marina's left eye was beginning to swell and darken with bruising.

Rose took Marina's head in her hands and tilted it for a better view. "You have a nasty gash which needs some butterfly stitches." Letting go of Marina's head she asked, "What happened?"

"I got hit by part of my tent whilst trying to put it up."

"I still don't get why you were erecting your own tent," complained Thabiti.

"For that you need to understand my family. I'm a young unmarried woman so I'm treated like a child. In fact, bossy cousin Elaxi and her husband went as far as suggesting I sleep in the children's tent. Just because they can't be bothered to look after their kids, why should I? But nobody disagreed with them, and my tent wasn't unpacked. So I decided to put it up myself. I have to admit I was pretty furious, and I think a tent pole took offence and hit me in the face." She smiled weakly.

"Thabiti, can you find your team's first aid kit?" Rose asked. "Then I'll need some ice wrapped in a tea towel or clean cloth."

"Ice out here?" questioned Chloe.

"In their cool boxes. Why, what did you put in yours?"

"Freezer packs."

Rose found steri-strips in the first aid kit and carefully placed two across the gash above Marina's eye to keep it closed and free from infection.

Rose heard a ringing sound and looked around.

Mayur answered his mobile phone. "Hi, Gautam. When will you be here?" Mayur listened to the person on the other end of the call. "What? Can't someone else deal with it?"

Mayur turned to his father. "Gautam said there's been some confusion with today's orders, and deliveries have been made to the wrong hotels and restaurants." He put the phone back to his ear and continued his conversation.

"Thank you, Lavanya," said Marina as the attractive Indian lady brought some ice, bundled in a tea towel.

Rose was about to place it on Marina's bruised eye when she heard Mayur declare, "I tell you, this was deliberate. Deepak Seth is bound to be behind it."

"Calm down," Kumar told Mayur.

Rose tipped Marina's head back and gently placed the improvised ice pack on her bruised eye.

Kumar clasped his hands together. "How could Deepak interfere with our deliveries? And if he did, it is more bad karma to add to his already hefty debt, which he will pay for in a future life."

"Karma and future life? What good are they? We need to take action against Deepak and his team now and deter them from further destructive action," argued Mayur.

"The only action we need now," stated Kumar, "is to find a winchman to replace your brother, and as he won't be bringing Isaac, we are short of a runner."

Marina twisted out of Rose's grasp. She stood and faced Kumar. "I'll be a runner," she cried.

"Sit down, Marina," Mayur spat dismissively. "This is serious."

"I am serious. I'm fit and run several times a week. And I've learnt a lot about topography during my work as a substitute lodge manager. Anyway, who else will you find at the last minute?"

"I'll go and ask around the headquarters." Mayur turned and began to walk away, but his father spoke.

"Thank you, Marina. I'm sure you are aware it is hot,

tiring work, and you have to be on the ball and observant at all times. Your team's safety will depend on it."

"No father," cried Mayur.

Marina beamed at Kumar. "Yes, Mr Chauhan. I promise I won't let you down."

"Well, you better continue with Mama Rose's treatment or you won't be able to see out of that eye."

Marina sat down and hugged Thabiti.

Rose watched as Mayur continued to argue with his father. Kumar eventually put a stop to it with a shake of his head and a look she could not discern. Mayur sat down next to Lavanya. She placed a hand on his arm, but he shrugged himself free.

Jono had remained silent during the exchange, staring into a bottle of Tusker and twirling his penknife. Rose could not see his eyes, yet a feeling of pain and self-pity swept over her. She felt cold. It must have been the ice she was holding. Once again, she took Marina's head and applied the ice pack. Marina was still grinning.

CHAPTER NINE

Thabiti volunteered to walk Rose, Chloe and Marina back to their respective camps. They walked past the registration tent and the large tent which now had "Bar" on a sign hanging above its entrance.

"Will you have to move your tent now that you're competing for the opposition?" Thabiti asked Marina. He chuckled.

"That's not funny." She playfully slapped his arm. "You're helping me move it if I have to."

"What does it matter where you camp?" asked Chloe.

"You've no idea the animosity my Uncle Deepak feels towards Kumar Chauhan. I hate to say this, but I agree with Mayur; it wouldn't surprise me if Uncle Deepak found a way to disrupt deliveries and keep two of Kumar's team in Nairobi."

"You are joking?" Chloe stopped.

"Not at all. Kumar used to work for my uncle and the Seths, until there was a family tragedy. After that, Uncle Deepak started mistreating workers and disappointing his customers. Kumar walked out and set up his own food import and wholesale distribution business. Actually, he's very successful, which only makes matters worse."

They began walking again, past the back of the Rusty Nail catering tent. Two men sat on plastic water containers, peeling potatoes.

"But what has this to do with Rhino Charge teams?" Chloe persisted.

"Everything. Uncle Deepak cannot compete with Kumar on a business level, so he tries to do so through the Rhino Charge. The trouble is, his team, Rhino Force, have only beaten Kumar's Bandit Bush Hogs once in the ten years they've both been competing."

They arrived at a gazebo and Rose looked up at a sign hanging across the top which read 'Rhino Force', printed in white lettering on a black background.

Marina commented, "Black is the colour of Rhino Force, the Seth family team."

They walked into a large camp with numerous tents erected around the perimeter, interspaced with 4x4 vehicles, which created a barrier between the camp and the rest of the headquarters.

Three children ran around with their African Ayah in close pursuit. A group of adults were seated in a large, grey, rectangular, marquee style tent. It was positioned in the centre of the camp and the front and one end were open.

"There she is," cried a stout middle-aged Indian lady. "Where have you been? You promised to play with the children and supervise their tea."

"Cousin Elaxi, I did not." Marina squared up to the lady.

"Well you're back now," an elderly Indian lady said. "Why don't you play football with the children? They love it when you do."

Marina looked down at the old lady with affection. "OK,

Mama." She picked up a football which was lying beside a chair and said, "But this is the last time I'm babysitting. I'm taking part in the Rhino Charge. I've a place on a team as a runner."

"What do you want to do that for, daughter?" said an elderly man who Rose presumed was Marina's father. "You're a lady, not some loutish boy. I forbid you."

"Now, now," soothed Marina's mother. "Let the girl have some fun. Why should she spend all weekend looking after someone else's children?"

Elaxi stood and stomped away.

A thin man with glasses sat apart from the group reading a book. "Good for you, cousin," he commented without looking up.

"Thank you, Aatma." Marina blushed.

"Well, as long as it isn't the Bandit Bush Hogs, I can't see her causing any harm." A fit looking man in his early seventies strode into the tent.

"Actually, it is them, Uncle Deepak."

The man's face reddened and he snapped, "I can't see what they want a girl for, anyway."

Two middle-aged men seated at the table smirked.

Marina turned to Rose, Chloe, and Thabiti. The three children approached her and the oldest attempted to grab the football she held. "Sorry about that. I'm afraid my family are not the most welcoming bunch. I suppose I'd better play with these kids. At least they appreciate me."

Thabiti leaned towards Marina and lowered his voice. "Will you be OK?"

She put a hand on his shoulder. "I'll be fine. I'm used to being on my own in this family."

CHAPTER TEN

Rose, Chloe, and Thabiti wandered through headquarters towards the officials' camp. The varied smells of numerous evening meals, being cooked on camp fires, blended in the air. The cries of children cut through the low murmur of chatter and there was a dull thud as a wooden mallet struck a metal tent peg.

Thabiti cleared his throat. "Was Pixel OK? Was she missing me?"

Rose laughed. "She's rather taken to Kipto, which is very sensible since she's the one who'll be feeding her."

"Oh that's a relief," said Thabiti. "Now, Jono told me you're sharing a tent and he put your stuff inside it."

"What do you make of Jono?" Rose asked.

Thabiti bit his lip. "I'm grateful he offered me a place on the team. The usual mechanic couldn't get time off from his job in the Congo."

Rose placed a hand on his arm. "Well, you've done him proud. I know how hard you've been working on that car." She stepped over a guy rope, but Chloe tripped and Thabiti caught her.

"Thanks. I think there's something melancholy about Jono," Chloe remarked.

"I know what you mean. In Nanyuki he was relaxed and often joked around, but here, particularly in our camp, he's quiet and detached from the rest of the group."

They arrived at the entrance to a fenced off area with 'Officials only' painted on a sign.

"Jono said your tent is the third one on the left," said Thabiti. They walked past red and grey-coloured mobile toilets and three small structures enclosed by green tarpaulins, above which white plastic containers were suspended with pipes dropping down.

Chloe raised her eyebrows.

"Showers," said Rose. "And I'm relieved the Portaloos are not too far from our tent."

They had a green canvas safari tent which had seen better days; there were a number of patches and Chloe had to fight the zip to open it. Their belongings were deposited on two iron bedsteads.

"Not bad," said Thabiti, peering inside. "At least you can stand up and move around which is more than I can in my little tent." He stood up. "I better head back. It's getting dark and I don't want to miss supper." He turned on a torch.

Rose and Chloe walked with him to their camp entrance. A large shape loomed out of the dusky light.

"Evening all," a voice drawled.

Thabiti laughed.

Rose pursed her lips and said, "Of course you're here as well, Sam."

"Wherever the action is, you can be sure to find two people: myself and Mama Rose." Rose scowled, but knew that he was correct. Recently, murder had followed them both around.

Sam was a large, muscular, bald-headed African man.

Rose was pleased they were friends otherwise she might be alarmed coming across him in the gloom. His ear and throat glinted in the torchlight. She hadn't noticed the gold jewellery before.

"Do you like my new earring? I needed a bit of bling." Sam turned his head towards Rose.

She replied, "I presume that's part of a disguise for one of your undercover missions with the Anti-Poaching Unit."

"Perhaps, but first I hear there's a vacancy for a strong man on one of the Charge teams."

Thabiti looked over at Sam and quickly looked away again. "Are you joining our team?"

"I sure am. I just spoke with Kumar, and even that rat of a son of his couldn't dispute that I'm a perfect match for the role. I'm your new winchman."

Thabiti shoved his hands into the pockets of his chino trousers and followed Sam back towards the Bandit Bush Hog's camp. Chloe and Rose returned to their tent.

"Time for a glass of vino," Chloe announced.

Rose sat down in one of the safari chairs placed outside their tent.

Chloe returned with a bottle of white wine and two plastic glasses. "Wow, what a day. There's been so much to take in." She poured wine into each glass, returned the bottle to the cool box, and slumped into the empty chair. "I think I understand what the Rhino Charge is. I even spotted different 4x4 vehicles as we walked through headquarters. But now I need to remember who everyone is. Let's start with the main officials." She took a large swig from her glass.

Rose began, "Christian Lambrechts is the Executive Director of Rhino Ark. That's the charity we discussed which finances the fencing projects. They are ultimately responsible for the Rhino Charge. We've not seen Christian yet, but he'll address competitors at the briefing, and hand out prizes at the end." She paused and sipped her wine.

Chloe declared, "We did meet Nick West and his bossy wife, Tanya."

"Shush," Rose implored. "They'll be staying in this camp, too." She caught Chloe's grin in the light of the paraffin lamp which an elderly African man placed outside their tent.

"Frank and Wendy Butler are the friendly, organised couple in the registration tent. More officials will arrive to man the guard posts."

Chloe stretched her legs out in front of her. "Then we met Thabiti's team, the Bandit Bush Hogs. I like Mr Chauhan but not his son, Mayur, as he's too fond of throwing his weight around."

Rose continued, "Nevertheless, he's driving this year. Thabiti is their mechanic and Jono the navigator. I'm happy for Marina as she's so excited Kumar included her in his team as a runner. Finally, there's Sam the winchman. I guess there must be another runner, but I don't know who that is."

"What does a runner do?" asked Chloe.

"Their job is to scout out the terrain ahead of the car, sometimes as far as a kilometre. They suggest possible routes to the driver and navigator, who ultimately decide where to go."

Chloe tucked a strand of hair behind her ear. "Then there is the team from Marina's camp, who call themselves Rhino Charge. The main man is her Uncle Deepak, who has a grudge against Kumar and is intent on beating him. So much so that he's flown a professional mechanic here from the UK."

"Well remembered. I think Deepak drives and the rest of his team is made up of family members. Probably the men we met. Of course, they didn't include Marina."

CHAPTER ELEVEN

R ose and Chloe were approached by an African man wearing a stained shirt. "Mama, Memsahib, supper will be ready at half past seven."

Chloe thanked him and said, "Poor Marina. I hope she'll be OK." She glanced at Rose. "Will Craig be all right without you?"

Rose thought of previous Rhino Charges with Craig and her throat felt thick. She replied hoarsely, "Kipto will be fussing over him and ordering Samwell to plump up his cushions. And he might appreciate some time by himself. Several times now I've caught him half asleep with an album of old photos on his knee, or dropped to the floor. Perhaps he's remembering the best bits of his life whilst he still can."

Rose sniffed and turned away from Chloe. She wiped her eyes with her sleeve and slurped her wine.

Chloe crossed her legs and changed the subject. "I wonder what Dan does when he's away. Whenever I ask him he either ignores my questions or tells me he's always working. But I'm sure he can't work all the time. He's not in the army now. Besides, I don't even know where he goes."

Rose wiped her eyes again and turned to Chloe. "I know

that most security people used to work for oil companies, but when the oil price collapsed at the end of last year, they lost their jobs."

Chloe frowned. "I don't think it's oil. He does gets very excited when those convoys of lorries pass through Nanyuki. You know the ones carrying large pieces of concrete and oversized airplane wings."

Rose smiled. "So does Craig. Those pieces are parts for the wind farm that's being constructed in Turkana. He thinks it's a fantastic idea to harness the ever-present winds of that area for power."

Chloe pursed her lips. "I suppose it's natural, like solar power, but I don't like wind or solar farms. They look ugly. In the UK there are loads of wind turbines, even in some of the most remote areas, and it spoils them." She sat up. "So Dan's probably in Turkana. Have you been there? What's it like?"

Rose considered the question. "It's the largest county in Kenya, but also the poorest, as it's semi-desert, and very hot and prone to draughts. Actually, I've only ventured up there a few times, to a campsite beside the lake. It's strange and beautiful in a moonscape way as the area surrounding the lake is mainly volcanic rock. And then there's Lake Turkana itself, which is very saline, and the winds, well, they are either a welcome relief from the heat or a relentless nuisance. Anyway, if you have the chance, it's worth visiting, but you have to take everything with you, and I mean everything, including a mobile fridge. There's no power, and no shops or restaurants."

"So what do you think Dan does all day?"

"He'll be in a large temporary camp which will have its own facilities and dining area, although I'm not sure about entertainment. I guess they rely on the internet."

Chloe grasped her wine glass. "No wonder he's started drinking again. It's not healthy for him, spending so much time on his own. And I think he drinks to help himself sleep, and forget."

"But you think it only makes matters worse? A kind of downward spiral," prompted Rose.

"Yes, that's exactly right."

Rose sat back and sipped her wine. She knew what Chloe was going through, but there was only so much she could do to help.

"Craig turned to the bottle after we lost the farm at Ol Kilima, and I thought he blamed me. After all, I was the one who shot the poacher and got us chucked out. I didn't understand at the time, but I do now. You see, he blamed himself for not being at the farm to protect me and Aisha, Thabiti's mum. Then he couldn't find another job, and I had to beg friends to lend us a small cottage. Of course, that just made matters worse. On the other hand, I became rather self-sufficient, although I was soon fed up of eating eggs from our chickens, and the rabbits which I'd shot. I tried to supplement them with vegetables and fruit, but it depended on what I grew or we were given. "

Chloe leaned forward. "But Craig's not like that now. What changed? How did he manage to get out of his rut?"

"I admit it took time. But once I got him out of the house, and he met a few people, he soon realised lots of them were in far worse predicaments. I suppose they always are in Kenya. Anyway, he was offered a job by a Kikuyu man who worked in Nairobi and owned a small ranch in Laikipia, which he was looking for someone to manage. Of course, most farm managers would dismiss such a job as they'd think it was beneath them. But for Craig, well, it was the boost he needed. For someone to have enough confidence in him to offer him a job. After that, life gradually improved."

Chloe sat up and crossed her arms. "I try to be bright and welcoming when Dan comes home. I even attempt to make his favourite dishes, cottage pie or roast chicken, and I'm not the world's greatest cook. Then I tell him about all the goings on in Nanyuki, and even suggest things we can do together while he's back."

Rose leaned towards Chloe. "I know you're trying to do the right thing, but I'm afraid you might actually be making things worse."

Chloe recoiled from Rose. "What do you mean? Why am I making them worse?"

"Can I have a touch more wine?" Rose asked. She watched Chloe reluctantly stand and fetch the wine bottle from the cool box inside the tent.

She topped up Rose's glass and repeated, "What do you mean? I don't understand."

"Thanks. Well, I've learnt my lessons the hard way, and when I think about Chris, I now realise how I should have treated him. Perhaps then we'd be on better terms."

"Your son?" interrupted Chloe, screwing the top back on the bottle. "Have you heard from him?"

"Oh, we've exchanged a few emails, and do you know, that's how I've worked out where I've been going wrong. I always wrote him these long letters telling him everything that was happening in Nanyuki, and all about the people he might know. His sister Heather loved it, she still does. But I don't think Chris did."

Rose paused so Chloe could return the bottle to the cool box. "When I think about it, why should Chris be bothered if Mrs so-and-so's cow develops Rift Valley fever or someone's son runs away with a local girl? No, what he wanted was for me to ask about him. And I don't mean the standard 'what are you doing?' questions. No, those that inquire about specific events and his feelings towards them, such as how are the boys in his dorm at school treating him? Do they make fun of him because he's from Africa?"

Rose placed her hand on Chloe's leg. "I think we women cope better with loneliness in our relationships. We tend to just do things and keep ourselves busy. Of course, this can make the situation worse, particularly if we come across as forceful and we push the men in our lives away from us."

Rose paused and then said, "I think they'd prefer that sometimes we stop and just ask them how they feel. We should make an effort to include them. The trouble is, we're so busy trying to keep our marriages and our families together, and do our work, that sometimes we just don't see this. You must remember, Dan is on his own a lot with too much time to think, so his loneliness, and being away from you, may make things worse."

"Wow," gulped Chloe. "I never thought of it like that. I've been so busy moving and trying to start a new life, which I've mostly done on my own, that I haven't really thought how leaving the army and the UK has affected Dan. And I get so down and worry each time I think I'm pregnant and then find out I'm not. So when I ask Dan what he's been doing and he just dismisses my questions, I get annoyed and offended. I just give up and go to bed. But I know he sits on his own and opens another bottle of wine because I find the empties in the morning. I guess it's a vicious circle, but if he won't talk to me, and won't answer my questions, how do I break it?"

Rose sat back and sipped her wine. "Can I suggest that instead of telling him what you've been doing, talk to him about how you're feeling. We can all throw tantrums and blame our husbands for how rubbish our lives are. But try to keep calm and make him feel wanted. Make sure he knows that his feelings and opinions matter."

Someone bashed a pan.

"Time for supper," announced Rose. She stood and linked arms with Chloe and together they walked towards the large mess tent.

CHAPTER TWELVE

Sam left Thabiti when they reached the bar tent in the centre of the headquarters. Thabiti felt conspicuous on his own, so he hastily made his way back to his own camp.

"Thabiti, there you are," called Mr Chauhan. "Come and join us for supper."

Under the events shelter, Mr Chauhan was seated at the head of the table with Jono on one side and Mayur on the other. He directed Thabiti to an empty seat next to Jono. There was a fifth place set at the foot of the table. Lavanya and two sweating African staff placed amazing looking Indian dishes on the table in front of him.

Thabiti breathed in their rich, spicy smells and his stomach ached. Lavanya pulled out the chair at the end of the table, but froze when Mayur shouted, "Woman, where are the chutneys and sauces?"

She dutifully left and returned carrying a metal tray on which were balanced small bowls of various coloured condiments. Jono sat silently staring down at the penknife he held in his clenched hands. Thabiti looked around and watched Mayur offer his father the dishes first, before helping himself and passing them on to Jono.

Thabiti waited impatiently, but Jono didn't pass him the bowls. Instead, he absentmindedly placed them on the table, so Thabiti reached over and started serving himself. He paused, looked at the other plates and resisted the urge to pile more onto his plate. He put his hand on his knife but felt a gentle pressure. Lavanya's dainty hand was on his, and as he looked across at her she gave a barely perceptible shake of her head.

Mr Chauhan, the palms of his hands together, recited, "Yagna shishta shinah shanto muchyante sarva kil bishaihi. Bhunjya tete tvagham papa, ye pachantyatma karnat." He nodded towards his guests and began to eat. Thabiti felt his stomach quiver as he looked around uncertainly.

Lavanya whispered, "You can eat now. Kumar said a simple prayer for our food which translates as, 'A righteous person who eats the food after it has been offered for sacrifice is released from all sins. The others who cook and eat solely for their own sake, eat sin'."

"That seems a little harsh, but I'm happy to eat and be released of my sins." Thabiti broke off a piece of chapati and dipped it in curry sauce. "Delicious," he exclaimed to Lavanya, who smiled shyly.

Kumar and Mayur talked animatedly, but Jono ate in silence, contemplating the chicken curry, rice and masala cauliflower on his plate. Thabiti twirled his fork. He didn't usually start conversations, and neither did Lavanya, it appeared. He glanced over at her and then down at his plate. "How long have you been married?"

"Thirteen years," she replied and forked some vegetable sambar into her mouth.

He was curious and realised he knew little of Indian customs despite living in Nairobi amongst a significant Indian population before moving to Nanyuki. Timidly, he asked, "Was it an arranged marriage?"

Lavanya pushed pieces of crispy green okra around her plate. "Yes, it was. My family are Shudras, or labourers, in the Hindu caste system. This is lower than the Chauhans who are the merchant class of Vaishyas. So when Kumar approached my parents, and told them he wanted a quiet, gentle-mannered wife for his son, they couldn't refuse. Even though they knew Mayur had a bad reputation and had been sent to work in London. You see, it brought them, indeed all my family, huge respect. Besides, I'm certain they received a substantial bride price from the Chauhans." She pushed her plate away.

"You've hardly eaten anything and this food is amazing." Thabiti was always hungry. "May I?" He indicated towards her plate and she nodded. He pushed his empty plate to one side, drew hers closer and began to eat. Lavanya was silent.

"Where are your kids?" He thought this a safe question. "Did you leave them in Nairobi?"

In a broken voice, Lavanya answered, "Mayur and I aren't able to have children."

Mayur must have heard her, as he shouted, "Barren dalit!"

Thabiti recoiled at the harsh words and Lavanya hung her head.

To his surprise, Jono pushed his chair back and jumped to his feet. Kumar extended his arm across the table. "Enough, Mayur." Kumar turned to Lavanya, whose head was still bowed. "Lavanya, my dear, thank you for a lovely meal."

"I'm going to the bar," announced Jono.

He marched out of the camp as a female voice Thabiti recognised shouted, "Careful!" A wavering light approached and Marina was revealed as she stepped into the mess tent. He had to shield his eyes until she turned off her head torch. "Hi, do you mind if I join you? It's not much fun in my camp," proclaimed Marina.

Mr Chauhan replied, "Of course, but I hope you don't

mind if I turn in. Lavanya, my dear, can you help me?"
Lavanya fetched Mr Chauhan's crutches and assisted him to
his feet.

"I'm going for a drink with Team 16," declared Mayur,
and strode into the night.

CHAPTER THIRTEEN

Thabiti and Marina sat down next to the glowing wood in the metal fire pit.

"Kahawa?" one of the African staff asked, and they nodded their acceptance.

"Coffee's OK, but I'd prefer a Tusker," mused Thabiti.

"Ah, I thought you might," Marina as she reached into her bag and triumphantly pulled out two tins of Tusker. "I grabbed these from Uncle Deepak's supply before I left."

"Cooee," shouted Chloe. "Do you mind if I join you? Bless her, Rose has gone to bed, but I'm just not sleepy."

Chloe sat down and removed a plastic wine glass and the half empty bottle of white wine from her bag. She lifted her head as Lavanya attempted to tiptoe past. "Come and join us around the fire," she called.

Lavanya looked timidly at them and then nodded.

"Wine?" Chloe offered, holding the bottle aloft.

Lavanya bit her bottom lip. "I don't usually, but perhaps just a little." She found an empty water glass on the dining table. "Please call me Lavi. Lavanya is rather formal and I prefer Lavi amongst friends. We are friends, aren't we?" she asked uncertainly.

"Of course," responded Chloe warmly. She lowered her voice and whispered, "Is Mayur your husband?"

Lavi nodded.

Thabiti poked the fire with a stick. "He was really rude to you at supper. Why is he like that?"

Lavi drew her glass to her chest. "He blames me. You see, we can't have children."

Chloe rested a hand on Lavi's knee. "You poor thing."

In the light of the fire, Thabiti spotted tears glistening in Chloe's eyes.

Lavi must have noticed the sympathetic note in Chloe's voice, as she turned to her and asked, "Do you have children?"

Rubbing her arm, Chloe answered, "No, I'm afraid I keep losing my babies. It seems my body reacts against the foetus and decides to expel it." Tears rolled down her cheeks.

Lavi placed a hand over Chloe's and squeezed. "I'm so sorry. I presume you've seen lots of specialists and have been examined, prodded and probed?" Chloe nodded. "I know what it's like. So have I. And the doctors found no reason that I can't conceive."

Lavi raised her head to look over Chloe's shoulder and then confided, "One whispered to me that it might be my husband who has the problem, but what can I do? He is an Indian man. There is no way he would tolerate a fertility test. And anyway, he would never admit if he was unable to have children. It would be seen as a weakness, a sign of failure." She shuddered.

"So instead he blames you?" Thabiti was both embarrassed and intrigued by this view into the world of women.

"Of course." Lavi gulped. "And he alternates between insulting and degrading me one minute, and threatening to send me back to my parents another."

Marina gasped.

Chloe wiped away her tears with her free hand. "I don't understand. Why is that an issue? At least you would be free of your vindictive husband."

Lavi hung her head, so Marina answered. "It's the shame, you see. Her whole family would be disgraced and what about her father and brothers? They all work for the Chauhan family. So they would either lose their jobs or be shunned by the other workers."

There was silence.

Then Chloe asked, "What about you Marina?"

Marina sat up. "What about me?"

"Well, firstly I'm intrigued by your name. Marina doesn't sound very Indian," Chloe commented.

Marina laughed. "Oh, it's not my real name. When I was little we visited relatives in India each year. Apparently, I insisted on swimming in the sea and visiting Marina Beach in Chennai. My cousins teased me about it, called me Marina and the name stuck. I like it, probably because it's not Indian and gives me my own identity."

"And do you live at home?" Chloe asked.

"I live with my parents and my brother Vijay Veejay. Both he and Baba work in the Seths' business, run by Uncle Deepak. You see, my mum is Uncle Deepak's youngest sister."

"So could you work in the family business?"

Marina laughed. "You saw how my family reacted when I told then I had a place in the Rhino Charge. There's no way I'd be accepted into the company, and anyway, it would be a nightmare working with my family. It's probably why I enjoy my safari work so much, as it gets me away from them all."

"Why don't you just move out?" Chloe probed.

Marina cried, "I can't afford Nairobi rents. And even if I moved to Nanyuki, I'm not offered enough work yet to support myself. It's rather embarrassing at my age having to still rely on my parents."

Chloe sipped her wine and asked, "What about finding more work? Or could you get a permanent job at a lodge?"

Marina raised her hands. "I'd love to and I've tried, but they usually want someone with more experience. Or a couple."

Thabiti had been following the conversation with interest, but now felt uncomfortable as if the girls were consciously trying not to look at him. He felt his face redden and quickly asked, "What about going to college or university? I'm trying to decide if I should go back and study."

Lavi said wistfully, "I loved university."

Thabiti looked at her in surprise. It was the first time she'd volunteered information. "What did you study?"

"Medicine. I wanted to be a doctor and help people."

"Oh, you must be clever," said Marina. "There's always so much competition for places to study medicine in Kenya, particularly amongst the Indian community. I'm afraid I was nowhere near bright enough."

Lavi blushed.

Thabiti was confused. He squinted at Lavi. "Are you a qualified doctor?"

Lavi bowed her head and shook it. "No, I didn't finish my course as I had to get married." Thabiti was about to ask why her marriage would stop her studying, but spotted Marina mouth "no" at him and shake her head. Embarrassed, he sank back into his chair.

Chloe tapped her legs. "I'm not very religious myself, unlike Rose who is a devout Catholic, but I know there are many Indian faiths. Do you participate in any?" Chloe looked from Lavi to Marina.

Marina locked eyes with Lavi and answered, "We are of the Hindu faith."

Lavi dropped her eyes and began to pick at a thread in her sari.

Marina crossed her ankles and continued, "It's a hard one for me. I've been brought up in the Hindu faith and I love the festivals like Diwali, the festival of light. And the numerous gods, particularly the goddess Durga. She represents the preservation of moral order and righteousness."

Marina gave Lavi a pitying look. "But where I struggle is that Hinduism defines a person's worth according to their position in a social hierarchy which is determined by birth. This means Lavi will always be considered inferior to my family because she was born into the Shudra caste of labourers."

Lavi looked up and murmured, "But that is because of karma. My spirit must have done something to displease the gods in my past life."

Marina shook her head. "You see I really struggle with that. I accept karma in that the actions I take have consequences, but it is my behaviour in the current life, which I have control over, that should count, not something that I did in a past life. And that is where I come into conflict with the Hindu religion. What do you think, Lavi?"

Lavi did not look up, but said softly, "I think there is no escape. I worked hard when I was young and I achieved a place to study medicine. But the gods made sure I didn't finish the course and they pulled me back to a life where I am just a wife. One who is ridiculed for not having children, so I have to spend my day cooking and looking after my husband and his family."

She looked up and smiled faintly. "But Kumar is good to me. And he lets me come on adventures like this one, to the Rhino Charge."

There was a further silence.

Chloe drained her glass and poured more wine. "I don't

mean to be rude, but I'm surprised there's such a large Indian community in Kenya. I hadn't expected it."

Marina grinned. "It's the fault of you British, but our history is fascinating. It started with trade at the end of the nineteenth century. Some Indian merchants had developed their own routes along the East African coast, but along came the British who set up an East African trading company in India. Soon afterwards, they moved the company to Mombasa, on the Kenyan coast, and they brought their Indian clerks and accountants with them. Do you know, the rupee was the first official currency in the British Colonial Protectorate? And it was run under Indian law."

Thabiti struggled to remember his colonial history lessons. "I thought lots of Indians died building the railway. Weren't they eaten by lions?"

"Oh, there were a pair of man-eating lions in Tsavo," agreed Marina.

Lavi piped up, "Two and a half thousand Indian workers died building the railway from Mombasa to Uganda. Of those who survived, some brought their families and settled here in Kenya. Of course, they weren't allowed to buy the best land, that was reserved for British farmers, but many became successful merchants and shopkeepers throughout the Kenyan Colony. By the 1920s, the Indian community was well represented on the legislative council." Lavi stopped and looked embarrassed.

"That's really interesting," encouraged Chloe. "And I have a feeling there's a but coming. What happened?"

Lavi looked at Marina who gave her an encouraging nod. "In the nineteen fifties, Indians were at the forefront of the campaign for increased rights. In fact, some Indian lawyers were probably linked to the African freedom fighters, better known as the Mau Mau. But at independence, the Indian economic dominance was too strong. So in an attempt to curb it, the new regime required Indians to apply for work permits, and then it banned them from trading in certain geographical areas. Many others lost their jobs and found their positions filled by Africans. Numerous families found they could no longer afford to live here, so they either returned to India or used their British passports to settle in the UK. The Asian population dropped by over fifty percent."

Marina opened her arms and pronounced, "So that's why our community has become so self-reliant, why we believe it's important to follow our traditions and customs. Of course, it might help if Indians are formally recognised in Kenya. I know there are members of our community who are pushing for us to become the forty-fourth Kenyan tribe." She looked wistfully into the fire. "I wish I could be more like Sonia Birdi."

"Why? Who's she?" Thabiti asked.

Marina playfully punched him. "Why, she's the first Indian woman to become a member of the Kenyan Parliament. After helping victims of the Sinai slum fire, she found a cause to fight for."

"She sounds inspirational," said Chloe, and patted Marina's leg. "Don't worry, you'll find your cause."

CHAPTER FOURTEEN

At eight o'clock on Sunday morning, Rose and Chloe stood at the back of the large bar tent where a stage had been erected at one end. In front of them the colour-coordinated Rhino Charge teams sat on folding chairs or stood around the edges of the tent.

"That's Christian Lambrechts," Rose whispered as a man spoke into the microphone. His voice retained a trace of his Belgian accent. "Welcome, everyone. There will be sixty-three teams taking part in the 27th Rhino Charge. I would like to thank the Mara North Conservancy for hosting this year's event." A ripple of applause spread through the tent.

"I would also like to thank you, the competitors, for taking part in the Rhino Charge and raising huge amounts of money for Rhino Ark."

There were cheers, jokes, and backslapping amongst the competitors. Christian passed the microphone to Nick West. "Morning, everyone. Today is scrutineering, where we check that your vehicles comply with the competition rules. Can each team drive to the collection point near the headquarters entrance? From there you will be directed to either the weigh-in, safety equipment test, or GPS system check. Scrutineering must be completed by five tonight, and the cars parked in the parc fermé. Any car not inside the secure enclosure by five will not take part tomorrow. You have been warned."

There were mutters in the crowd. "Finally," said Nick, "team briefing will commence at five pm, when the competition maps will be handed out. Thank you." Nick placed the microphone back in its stand, but then removed it. "Officials meeting in ten minutes." He left the stage.

Rose and Chloe waited and watched the teams file out. Thabiti and Marina gave them a wave. The bruising under Marina's eye had turned a dark purple. They all wore bright blue t-shirts and Sam's strained over his muscular chest. Deepak's team looked menacing in all black.

Rose and Chloe wandered into the centre of the tent and were about to sit down when Wendy Butler approached them. "Morning, ladies. Did you sleep well?"

"Morning Wendy," answered Rose. "Yes, thank you."

"I don't think you were given your officials polo shirts yesterday."

Rose and Chloe followed Wendy to the stage. Wendy held a shirt up in front of Chloe, tutted and found two smaller ones. "These should fit you. You need to wear one today, for the scrutineering, and the other is for tomorrow."

CHAPTER FIFTEEN

T he Bandit Bush Hog's camp was in an uproar. The safety equipment which Chloe had handed out at registration the previous afternoon was missing.

Mayur shouted at his father, "Don't you understand? Someone is deliberately trying to prevent us from taking part. You have to stand up to the Seths and show them you won't be intimidated."

Kumar rested wearily on his crutches. "Mayur, why do you get so angry? And you always blame someone else. I'm sure there is a perfectly simple explanation and we will find the equipment has just been mislaid."

Marina appeared from one of the sleeping tents. "Nothing in here."

Lavi and the African staff searched the events shelter with Jono's ineffectual assistance.

Thabiti walked across to the team's car. It was best to look busy and although he had run through everything yesterday, there was no harm checking the car again. At least it would keep him out of the girls' way.

He sat in the driver's seat. As Sam appeared, Thabiti switched on the ignition. Nothing. Sam's eyes widened.

Thabiti tried again. He felt his pulse race. The car had started immediately yesterday.

Sam leaned into the car. "Don't trouble Kumar or mention this to Mayur just yet. Go over the car again. In particular, check all the leads and wires in case something has shaken loose during transportation."

Sam's tone was clear and calming and Thabiti felt his heartbeat steady. "I'll start by looking under the bonnet."

"While you do that," said Sam, "I'll check that the safety equipment wasn't left behind in the registration tent yesterday afternoon."

Thabiti unlatched the bonnet of the vehicle and secured it in place. From his tool kit he extracted a small torch and peered into the back of the engine. Everything looked secure, but he instinctively knew something was out of place. What was it? He touched the panel protecting the starter motors. It wobbled and the bolts securing it were loose. He lifted the panel and the problem was clear: four electrical connectors hung free.

Thabiti stood up and looked around. Kumar was sitting in the events shelter. Mayur and Jono had their heads bowed in discussion, and the search party must have reached the staff area, behind the thorny bushes, as Thabiti heard clangs and shouts.

Thabiti reached for his phone and photographed the offending connectors. He secured them in place just as Sam strode back into camp through a gap in the leleshwa bushes.

"Panic over," exclaimed Sam. He reached Kumar and was joined by Mayur and Jono.

Marina dashed round from the cooking area. "Have you found everything? Where were they?" she asked breathlessly.

"As none of the officials had seen them, I decided to wander around the headquarters. I met some children waving emergency flags and asked them to show me where they'd found them. It was behind some mobile toilets and the other equipment was still there."

"That's a huge relief." Kumar's voice was shaky.

"I know Deepak Seth is sabotaging our team," exclaimed Mayur.

Jono asked, "What about the numbers?"

"I have those," Thabiti shouted. He wiped his hands on a cloth and reached into the car through the passenger door. He brought out three numbers: one for either side of the car and a large one to be placed on the roof.

"I'll help Thabiti stick them on," Sam volunteered. When he reached Thabiti, he whispered. "Have you found the starter problem?"

"I think so." Thabiti showed Sam the photo of the disconnected cables.

"That's no accident. Have you tried to start it again?" Sam asked.

"Not yet." Thabiti gingerly hoisted himself into the driver's seat. His mouth was dry as he turned the key in the ignition. The vehicle spluttered to life. He turned the engine off and sat back, feeling giddy.

CHAPTER SIXTEEN

Thabiti's sister, Pearl, was trying to read a magazine, sitting up in bed in the Cottage Hospital in Nanyuki. She was twenty-four, slim and attractive, but after the traumatic circumstances surrounding her mother's death, she had stopped eating and become very weak.

She began her recovery in the Cottage Hospital and then returned home to Guinea Fowl Cottage, which she shared with her brother. But her health began to deteriorate as Thabiti spent more time working at Mr Obado's garage.

Dr Farrukh, the female member of a work and marriage partnership, suggested she return to the Cottage Hospital for observation while Thabiti was at the Rhino Charge. Reluctantly, Pearl agreed, when she realised their house girl, Doris, would be taking a much-needed week's leave.

Images from Pearl's childhood replayed in her mind. How had these led up to the recent upsetting events? And what was she going to do now? What had she to look forward to? She sank back into her pillows.

Dr Farrukh stepped into the ward through the patio doors at the far end. They had been opened to allow fresh air and a cool breeze into the stuffy ward. Dr Farrukh strode up to

Pearl. "I really think you need to start exercising. How about something gentle at first, like yoga? This afternoon there is a group session in the garden. It starts at four o'clock. Why don't you join them? At the very least, you'll get some fresh air."

Pearl leant her head to one side and considered the proposal. She was bored of reading magazines and some sun on her face would be refreshing. She wasn't sure about yoga. That was for skinny white women who ate muesli and drank kale shakes.

She looked up at Dr Farrukh's set expression. "OK. I'll give it a try." Anything to get rid of the woman and her alternating looks of pity and disapproval. She supposed yoga didn't sound too strenuous.

She dressed in a black sleeveless t-shirt and leggings over which she wrapped a yellow striped kikoi, so it formed a wrap-around skirt. She poked her feet under the bed until she located her leather, beaded flip-flops. Grabbing the magazine, she strolled out of the patio doors into the garden.

The yoga class hadn't started, so she curled up on a nearby bench, in the dappled shade of a jacaranda tree. Her mind drifted with the sweet honey smell of the blossoms and the trickling of the Nanyuki river, meandering across its pebble bed beyond the tree.

She felt light-headed, but she was also relieved that her thoughts weren't jostling for attention. She closed her eyes and continued to drift with the bubbling water.

A female voice disturbed her. "Excuse me. I hope you don't mind," said a nurse, "but Mr Kariuki always sits here in the afternoon." Pearl uncurled her legs as the nurse assisted an elderly African man onto the bench and told him, "I shall be back in an hour."

Pearl opened her magazine, but she couldn't concentrate.

Instead, she stared at Mount Kenya, just visible through a break in the tree line.

"You feel its power, don't you, my dear?" Pearl jumped. The old man's voice was soothing but strong. "You are a Kikuyu?"

"I am, but I don't believe in the old religion."

"Oh. What do you believe in?"

Good question. She didn't really believe in anything and certainly not people, as they had a habit of letting her down.

The old man didn't seem to expect an answer. "The mountain is a holy place. Many believe Ngai, the creator of all things, inhabits it when the cloud descends and covers its peak. Do you feel its strength? Do you feel the life forces in every animal, plant and object around you?"

Pearl crossed her legs. She wasn't sure she could put up with the old man's ramblings.

He seemed to read her thoughts and he chuckled. "Why are you here?" he asked. "There is nothing wrong with you."

Pearl crumpled her nose and said in an airy voice, "I've been through a difficult time. Dr Farrukh wants to keep an eye on me."

The old man chuckled again. Pearl felt her eyes and cheeks burn. "You are hiding. All your life other people have run about for you, provided for you, and made decisions for you."

Pearl turned to the old man, pursing her lips, and saw that his eyes were dull and ghostly. She jumped back. He was blind.

"I don't need my eyes to see these things. I feel your pain, your confusion and your uncertainty. Your mind is disconnected from your body and your spirit. What is your purpose in life?"

Purpose? She didn't have a purpose. Her whole body felt

hot. This blind old man had no idea what she'd been through, how she'd suffered.

He continued, "We all have a purpose in life. Without it we would drift and feel no connection to other people or ourselves."

Pearl felt her throat thicken. She was not going to cry. Not because of a few words from this old man. He was right, though. She was no use to anyone. What had she to look forward to in life? Nobody liked her the way she was. They always wanted something from her.

Mr Kariuki asked, "Are you Aisha Onyango's daughter?"

Here we go, thought Pearl. Comparing me to my brilliant mother. A mother who was never content with Pearl's poor grades or understood why her school reports always described her as 'distracted'. She was not clever like her Mama. She would never be a leading lawyer who spoke out against corruption and inequality in Kenyan society.

"Then you are descended from Anjiru, daughter of Gikuyu and Mumbi. So am I, and our clan is renowned for both great warriors and mundu mugo, healers. Your mother was a warrior. Which are you?"

"You may have known my mother and all the amazing things she did, but I am neither a warrior nor a healer."

The old man grasped her hand and Pearl resisted the urge to yank it away. He opened her palm and traced the lines on it. "You have the strength to be both, if you decide to harness and direct it."

Pearl pulled back and held both hands to her chest.

"Ah, your yoga class has started. Join them and begin to harness your inner strength. Perhaps we can continue our talk another day?"

I don't think so, thought Pearl.

CHAPTER SEVENTEEN

The buzz of suppressed excitement was almost tangible as Rose and Chloe entered the large bar tent.

It was just after five o'clock. They had spent all day checking car licences and safety equipment, and were now tired and covered in dust.

Nick West tapped the microphone as he stood on the stage at the far end of the tent. A hush descended and people either sat down or turned to face him.

"Firstly, thank you, everyone, for completing the scrutineering in such good time, and for allowing us to sort out a few technical snags we had with the GPS equipment. I'm delighted to confirm that all sixty-three cars are parked in parc fermé, ready for tomorrow's competition."

"Now, before I hand out the maps, I have a few house-keeping points. Remember, the maximum speed limit, even on flat ground, is forty kilometres per hour. We will know if you exceed this."

"Next, Amref will be providing medical cover tomorrow, so please ensure you have handed in your membership forms. If you still need to complete a form, they will be available after this briefing at the Amref stand, opposite the catering area. There will be a plane on standby at Wilson airport tomorrow just in case someone suffers a major injury."

As Nick continued running through event information, Rose looked around. It was a strange event, pitching man and their machines against nature, and yet it generated huge enthusiasm, passionate rivalry between teams, and large amounts of money for wildlife conservation.

She and Craig shared so many wonderful memories from past Rhino Charges, but she knew she would have to start thinking about life without him.

She so hoped he would not deteriorate further, not before Heather's summer visit. And she prayed Chris would travel from England soon to see his father. Their relationship with Chris was still very fragile.

She knew she was lucky to have so many friends in the community. Admittedly, some of her contemporaries were beginning to fall ill and some had already died. But at least she had the youth and enthusiasm of Chloe and Thabiti to ensure she didn't wallow in self-pity.

She still enjoyed her role as a community vet, although some of the work was becoming harder, as she wasn't as strong as she used to be. And her knobbled, arthritic hands made tasks like stitching difficult.

She smiled to herself. Still, she was lucky as she was never truly alone. Every week she met a friend or two in town for coffee, and people often called at the house with some fruit or vegetables that they'd grown.

At home, she had her myriad of animals and the support of her staff who helped look after them, herself and Craig. And who in their mid-sixties had the opportunity to be involved in such an iconic event as the Rhino Charge?

She heard Nick West say, "So to round up. You are to

arrive at parc fermé from half past five tomorrow morning and be ready, from a quarter to six, to be escorted to your starting guard post. Can one member from each team collect a competition map? Thank you."

CHAPTER EIGHTEEN

R ose sat outside her tent in the officials' camp. Chloe had ventured over to the safari showers to try them out, so for the first time that day, Rose had some time to herself. She decided to call Craig.

"Hi, it's me," she said into her mobile phone. "Am I disturbing you?"

Craig answered, "No. Not at all. It's lovely to hear your voice. I'm just waiting for Kipto to finish preparing my supper, although I'm not sure what she's cooking."

"So she and Samwell are looking after you? And did Dr Farrukh visit yesterday?"

"Yes, and she checked my blood pressure, but there's no change. She's visiting again on Tuesday. So how is the Rhino Charge?"

"It's not the same without you, although Chloe is good company, and Thabiti is excited about tomorrow. Big Sam has joined his team… "

Craig interrupted, "That man turns up like a bad penny. But I'm glad he's on Thabiti's team and can keep an eye on him."

Rose continued, "Most of the usual characters are here,

including the Butlers who are keeping us all organised. It's very dry, so the drivers' concerns are the loose sandy ground. It won't be like the last time when you and I were here, and the cars were all getting stuck in the mud or slipping off tracks. Do you remember we had to get towed into camp that year?"

She heard Craig chuckle at the end of the line and say, "But oh, what a party we had when the Bennetts won the trophy."

She asked, "Have you had any visitors?"

"Dickie Chambers popped by yesterday afternoon to discuss polo. And he filled me in with the latest politics and carryings-on over a beer. Apart from that it's been rather quiet. I suspect most people are down with you."

"I've certainly seen some familiar faces, but we've been busy. Scrutineering today was particularly tiring in the heat."

"I better go, old bean. Kipto's just put my supper on the table and Samwell is hovering in the doorway to help me. Look after yourself."

"And you."

CHAPTER NINETEEN

C hloe and Rose emerged from their tent just before half past five on Monday morning. It was the 2nd of May, which was a public holiday across Kenya as May 1st, which was Labour Day, had been a Sunday.

Chloe stamped her feet and hugged herself. "I'm pleased you told me to bring some warm clothing." She wore a lightweight down jacket, with the hood up to keep her head warm, and leather gloves.

Last week Rose had used the upcoming event as an excuse to visit Mitumba: a large market of second-hand clothes exported from Europe. At a stall specialising in fleece items she had haggled with the stall holder for a gilet, jacket, hat and gloves. The colours might be mismatched, but she felt very cosy.

Chloe yawned and picked up her bag. The camp staff had prepared a flask of hot water and given them sachets of tea and coffee, and a small carton of milk.

As they walked past the large bar tent towards parc fermé Chloe exclaimed, "The whole of headquarters must be awake, and half the Mara." Tall spotlights shone down on the parked vehicles and people were everywhere, like a swarm of multi-coloured locusts.

There was a lot of shouting, banging, and general excitement. Even Rose felt a flutter of anticipation in her empty stomach.

"Good luck," shouted Chloe to the Bandit Bush Hogs as they stalked past. Their blue t-shirts were supplemented with yellow accessories: a beanie hat for Thabiti, a rope-like belt for Jono and yellow jackets all round. Marina and Thabiti acknowledged the greeting by raising their hands, but neither smiled, and Marina's bruise appeared a deep black. They must be nervous, thought Rose. It was their first Rhino Charge.

Only Sam, who strode causally at the back, called to them. "Morning, ladies. Now make sure you keep out of trouble."

"We have to find the vehicle driving to guard post seven," said Rose. They looked around.

Chloe tapped Rose's shoulder. "Someone's holding a number seven flag over there next to the vehicle with 'Sandstorm Kenya' printed on the side and a lizard logo." They were directed to a fawn-coloured Land Cruiser. After ten minutes, a car with a number eight flag drove out of the headquarters, followed by five Rhino Charge vehicles.

"We leave next," their African driver told them as he started the engine. Their journey was slow and bumpy, but Chloe was delighted to spot something moving through the grass beside the track.

Leaning forward between the front seats, she asked the driver, "What's that?"

"A serval cat," he answered. "It has a small head, but big ears." Rose looked out of the window. The serval cat was larger than a domestic cat and had long legs. Rose only caught brief glimpses of its tan-coloured body and dark spots, as it was well-camouflaged in the dry grass.

"How much longer?" moaned Chloe, settling back in her seat.

"Ten minutes, Madam. We are heading to guard post seven, which is one of the furthest from headquarters. But don't worry, you will see lots of action because you are at one end of the Gauntlet."

"The Gauntlet," Frank Butler briefed them on arrival at their guard post, "is a combination of guard posts five, six and seven. There will be a lot of spectators as the route down that rocky outcrop over there will probably determine the winning teams."

After Frank completed his briefing, Chloe poured hot drinks. A team from Sandstorm Kenya, who were sponsoring the guard post, unpacked water and food. Rose and Chloe strode to the bottom of a rocky slope.

"Cars can't possibly drive down here." Chloe's eyes widened as she looked up the incline. "There's a huge boulder in the way and the surface is covered in jagged rocks, which are far too large to drive over. And bushes are growing in all the crevices."

Rose leaned her head to one side, "Oh, they will, and the bushes won't last long." They walked around to the side of the outcrop which faced the guard post.

"This might be the most direct route, but it's far too steep and look at those rock ledges."

Rose chuckled, "Just wait and see. Teams won't just drive down this slope, some will also attempt to drive up it."

Chloe unzipped her jacket as the day was beginning to heat up. "What is this Gauntlet Frank was telling us about?"

Rose paused, "I suppose it could be described as a mini Rhino Charge. As with the main competition, the winner is the team which reaches the three checkpoints in the shortest distance. Usually the course has some of the most difficult obstacles on the whole Charge and invariably there's a water crossing. Frank is right, though. There will be a lot of spectators. We will need to manage them and keep them off the course. We don't want any accidents."

CHAPTER TWENTY

R ose stood inside the guard post tent and watched the rally clock. It was synchronised with headquarters and clicked towards half past seven, the starting time for the Rhino Charge. Chloe waited outside. At twenty-nine minutes past seven, Rose raised her hand and Chloe replicated the action by raising the number seven flag.

The clock clicked to seven-thirty. As Rose dropped her hand, Chloe swept the flag to the ground in a theatrical gesture as if she was starting a formula one motor race.

Wonda, one of the Sandstorm Kenya representatives, ticked off the five teams, starting at the guard post, on a clipboard. Rose joined Chloe and they watched two teams turn north.

"They're taking the easier route," commented Rose. "I presume they'll hope to have enough time at the end of the day to complete the Gauntlet."

"The other three teams are tackling the slope." Chloe bounced up and down on the soles of her feet. "Oh," she cried disappointedly. "Car 11 is taking the easy option."

They watched as it drove a circuitous route around the outcrop and up a gentler incline.

Car 54, a compact red Land Rover, waited at the bottom of the easier rocky slope. "Are those the runners?" Chloe asked.

"Yes," answered Rose as she watched three red-topped team members grapple their way up the easier slope. "See how they move aside bushes as they scout for the best route." One turned and waved a white cloth. The driver must have been waiting for the signal as the car rolled forward.

The gathering crowd groaned and Rose stiffened when the car lost traction and began to slide backwards, sending a cascade of stones downhill. It ground to a halt, altered course to the right, and carefully continued its climb.

"Their car sounds like a wild beast," said Chloe. "The engine growled and grunted as it climbed, and now it's reached flatter ground at the top it sounds as if it's purring."

Applause from the crowd sent Car 54 on its way and Rose's attention was diverted to Car 18, which was still at the bottom of the steepest slope. She and Chloe walked forward so they had a better view of the yellow and black vehicle with 'Bundu Bandits' painted on the side.

"Can you see the winch cable running from the front of the car up the slope?"

"No," Chloe scowled. A figure appeared at the top of the slope and waved towards the driver. The winch cable tightened and very steadily, Car 18 began its climb.

Chloe gasped. "I see what you mean now." Halfway up the slope, the car began to slip back until the winch cable became taught and held it in place.

"The winch not only stops the car sliding backwards, it actually pulls it over the most demanding sections," Rose instructed Chloe.

"It's taking ages, though. I know you said the winner doesn't have to be the quickest around the course, but surely Car 18 will never reach all the checkpoints at this pace."

Chloe leaned forward as the car drove and was then dragged by the winch over a rock ledge. She exhaled as it completed the manoeuvre.

"This team may not be trying to win the main event. You see there's a separate trophy for the winner of the Gauntlet." After several more tense minutes, Car 18 reached the top and the crowd whooped and literally danced for joy.

"They appreciated that," said Rose. "Watch out, here comes the first team from another guard post."

Rose called to the Sandstorm crew who were still watching Car 18. They rushed into the tent, reappearing with bottles of water, fruit and hand-operated water sprays. "Those are like the sprays I use for my house plants," commented Chloe.

Car 44 progressed steadily down the hill. "Gravity helps this vehicle," observed Chloe. "The momentum of its own weight helps it climb over the largest boulders and the driver has a much greater ability to pick his course." Her hand flew to her mouth. "I see what you mean about the bushes. That car completely flattened them, and it's about to arrive."

A storm of dust rose into the air as Car 44 reached flat ground, sped towards the guard post and braked hard. "Are we clear to proceed?" the driver asked, refusing the bottle of water he was offered. Rose nodded.

The runners, whose red faces matched their t-shirts, allowed the Sandstorm team to give them a final spray of water before they dashed off, overtaking their vehicle. Another team member, standing in the back of the car, waved at them.

The bonnets of two teams appeared at the top of the slope simultaneously. Car 57 began its descent, but it was too fast. The front of the car lurched to the left and hit a large boulder. The driver must have attempted to reverse, as the wheels spun backwards, but the car didn't move. It was stuck. Car 1, painted bright yellow, inched between Car 57 and the trunk of a tree and reached the bottom of the slope, becoming the second car through the guard post.

Chloe grabbed Rose's arm. "Is that Marina's Uncle Deepak's team?" Rose could see the outline of a car at the top of the steep slope. Zigzagging down it were three Indian men wearing black shirts. They turned and scrambled back up the slope. Rose read 'Rhino Force' and '63' on the back of their shirts.

"Deepak must be brave." Chloe bobbed up and down in excitement as she watched. "There's no way I'd attempt to drive down that slope, and he must be in his late sixties. No offence meant," she said, giving Rose a sideways glance.

"None taken." There was a lot of shouting from the Rhino Force team and then the nose of the car dropped over the edge. Rose heard a collective gasp from the swelling crowd of onlookers and Chloe beside her. She felt her own throat constrict as she watched Car 63 inch its way down the slope towards them.

"Can you see? They're using the rear winch to restrain the vehicle as it descends."

The crowd surged forward.

Rose placed a hand on Chloe's arm. "We need to push these spectators back to a safe distance. Any minute, another car could speed around the side of the rocks and drive straight into them." Chloe and Rose waved their arms and shooed people back.

The Rhino Force car jolted onto flat ground. "Ow! That must have hurt," cried Chloe.

Marina's Uncle Deepak drove the car to the guard post and got out. He rolled his neck and stretched his arms. As each of the team members gulped water or chewed pieces of watermelon, Deepak grunted, "Well done team. Keep it up. Now for the next section I need you, Aatma, to go far ahead with Vijay, to find the best route to the next guard post. Hinesh, you keep close and call out if I'm about to hit anything or drive into a hole."

Two Indian men sped away as Deepak climbed back into the vehicle. A middle-aged man Rose had seen in their camp climbed into the passenger seat and they drove north.

CHAPTER TWENTY-ONE

Thabiti felt adrenaline pump through his body. He stood on the side of a slope, wondering how Mayur would push through the thicket of bushes surrounding them without landing on a rock or hitting a tree.

"Thabiti," Marina called. "We need your help finding a route through this." Mayur stopped the car as Marina and Thabiti pushed aside bushes and examined the ground up the right-hand side of the slope. Jono and George, the other runner, mirrored their actions on the left and Sam was higher up the slope. Sam waved his arms and shouted, "You want to aim for me. This is the clearest route once you're through the bushes."

Thabiti and Marina moved across the slope and positioned themselves between the vehicle and Sam. Marina found a large boulder and climbed on top of it. Waving her arms she shouted, "If you aim to the left of me you should be OK."

Thabiti tripped. "Watch out for this tree trunk," he called. He clenched his hands and kept glancing away as Mayur carefully, but boldly, drove the car up the slope. Mayur was a good driver and he quickly altered course when the car met a rock which was too large to drive over.

As the car passed between him and Marina, Thabiti watched the determined and focused expression on Mayur's face. How could he see where he was going? Thabiti gasped as the car barged its way through the thick foliage.

They all reached guard post six which was on top of a cliff. Thabiti rested his hands on his hips and panted.

"Just look at this view." Marina pointed into the distance. "That's the Mara River winding its way through the reserve, while the crocs lie in wait for one of the famous wildebeest crossings."

Mayur and Jono spread a map on the car bonnet. Jono traced a route with his finger. George and Sam had vanished.

"I'm not in as good a shape as I thought I was," wheezed Thabiti. "I've spent too much time working on the car rather than on my fitness."

"Unlike Sam, who despite his size hasn't stopped moving," marvelled Marina. "I think he's taken George to scout the next section. I'd better join them."

Jono called to Thabiti, "Do you want to hitch a lift in the back for the next section?"

Gratefully, Thabiti climbed aboard and firmly grasped a metal rail as the car bounced over the rocky escarpment. He jumped down when they came to a stop at the top of a steep slope and joined his teammates.

"That's guard post seven down there, which is the end of the Gauntlet. If we're to stand any chance of winning, this is the route we'll have to take," declared Mayur. "Other vehicles have come this way. I can see their tracks."

"I don't think that's a good idea," Jono argued. "This slope is extremely steep and uneven, and there are some nasty rock ledges to catch us out."

Mayur turned to Sam. "Will you be able to steady my descent with the rear winch?"

Sam nodded. "I've already found a couple of sturdy trees. I'll wrap the winch strop around them and secure the winch cable to it."

Jono paled. "I really think we ought to check out alternative routes."

Sam slapped him on the back. "Don't worry, my friend. We can do this if we work together as a team." He called to Thabiti, "Fetch me the winch strop. You know, the yellow length of nylon webbing."

Thabiti lifted the lid of a metal box which was bolted to the floor in the back of the vehicle. He found the winch strop and ran over to Sam, who wrapped it round two sturdy trees. He handed the looped ends to Thabiti.

Next, Sam drew out the rear winch cable until it reached where Thabiti stood. He unscrewed the D-ring shackle, threaded the curved section through both ends of the winch strop, and screwed the pin back in place. He tugged the winch strop and grunted in satisfaction.

"Thabiti, stand at the top of the slope so you can relay instructions from Mayur and the team below. I think we'll find a warm welcome from Mama Rose and Chloe at the bottom."

Sam picked up a control box and walked as far as the control cable would allow. He clicked a button and the winch spun slowly until the cable was taught. "I'm ready," shouted Sam.

Mayur drove Car 27 over the edge of the slope.

CHAPTER TWENTY-TWO

Rose bit into a cheese and ham roll. She needed to maintain her strength.

Chloe ran into the tent, her eyes sparkling. "The Bandit Bush Hogs are here and they're attempting the steeper slope."

Rose wiped crumbs from her mouth, grabbed a bottle of water, and hurried after Chloe. They stood in front of the spectators who were once again edging closer to the action. Jono was towards the bottom of the slope, pacing this way and that. Marina was below the car, gesticulating to Mayur, and Thabiti stood higher up and appeared to be relaying instructions to whoever was at the top of the slope.

"They're using the winch." Chloe was bobbing up and down again.

"That means Sam must be at the top and Thabiti's passing him instructions."

The car made good progress as Marina assisted Mayur to navigate around the worst crevices and boulders. It reached a point about five metres from the bottom of the slope where there was an imposing ledge.

"That's a steep drop." Chloe tapped her hands against her legs.

"Don't worry, with the winch to hold it, the car will pop over the edge and then they'll be down," Rose reassured her.

Mayur drove over the ledge. The back of the car reared up. Thabiti dived to the ground. Rose heard the metal winch cable whip through the air. The crowd gasped.

Rose shouted, "Marina, get out of the way." Marina was grabbed and hauled back by the other runner as Car 27 flipped over, bounced, and flipped again, landing on its roof at the bottom of the slope.

There was an eerie silence, broken by the sound of dislodged rocks as Sam sped down the slope. He flung himself to the ground next to the driver's door, and yanked free the window cage. He reached into the car.

"Quick, get the medic," Rose instructed Chloe. "Then radio headquarters. I think they'll need to call in the Amref plane." She ran forward, but stopped. "And send someone with the backboard."

The Bandit Bush Hog team gathered around the car whilst the Sandstorm representatives held the spectators back. Sam took charge. He used his immense strength to pull the car door open and wrestled it from its hinges. He lay face down on the ground and poked his head inside the car.

"Mayur, can you hear me? Mayur." Rose thought she heard a grunting sound. "It's OK, Mayur. The car's flipped over and you're upside down, but you're safe. I'll get you out, but you have to stay still and do exactly as I tell you."

Rose felt some of the tension leave her body. Mayur was alive and conscious. She could hear his voice, but not make out the words. Sam jumped to his feet as the medic arrived and Wonda panted to a stop carrying a backboard.

"He's conscious and can feel his feet, although he says his arm throbs." Sam looked at Wonda. "Do we only have one backboard?"

"Yes," the medic answered.

Rose turned as the 'Pink Ladies' car stopped beside them. "Can we help?" the driver asked.

"Do you carry a backboard?" asked Sam.

She wrinkled her mouth. "No, but we have a length of timber to help us over rough terrain."

"That might do."

One of the pink-clad ladies pulled a four-foot length of wood, just wider than a car wheel, from the back of their car.

Sam bounded around to the passenger side of the upside-down car and pulled at the door, which resisted but finally scraped along the ground.

"George," Sam instructed the other runner. "Bring that piece of wood here." George knelt by the open passenger door and Sam did the same at the driver's side. "Carefully push the plank through to me, underneath Mayur's legs. Steady with the end." Sam reached in and grabbed the end of the wood. "Hold it there, George. Thabiti, hold this end still."

Chloe arrived and pulled Rose to one side. "Headquarters are sending a vehicle, but it will take at least twenty minutes to reach us. Do you mind if I borrow the medic for a minute? It's Jono. He's in a real state. I don't think he's actually broken anything, but he is covered in cuts and bruises, and when I tried to help him stand, he collapsed." Chloe escorted the medic to where Jono sat on the ground, curled into a ball.

She returned and said, "I think we should go. There are teams arriving from both directions."

"Of course," said Rose. She admonished herself. Come on, old girl. No point standing around here. It looks like Sam knows what he's doing, and you've work to do. Rose and Chloe left as Sam, with Marina's assistance, slid the backboard at an angle under Mayur's head . Rose was not sure if Mayur was still conscious.

"At least the engine stopped when the car did," said

Chloe. "A fire on top of the accident is the last thing we need."

"I think we can thank Sam's quick thinking for that. I'm sure he hit the kill switch on the ignition the moment he reached the car."

Wonda had returned to the guard post, and her team offered the team of Car 14 refreshments. The spectators kept glancing across at the upside-down Car 27, but their attention was drawn back to another team negotiating the easier slope.

Rose and Chloe, with Wonda's assistance, checked three more teams through the guard post, including the Pink Ladies, before Frank Butler and a second Land Cruiser arrived from headquarters.

"This is a most unfortunate business, Rose. Can you tell me what happened?" Rose described the events she had witnessed. As she finished, the Bandit Bush Hog team descended on the guard post. Jono limped in, supported by George. He was pale and covered in cuts and scrapes which Rose presumed were from hitting the ground, although she couldn't remember seeing him in the path of the car.

A dusty Sam, with grazed knees, carried one end of the backboard whilst Thabiti, who had blood seeping through his trousers, and Marina, with her black eye, struggled with the other end.

"Can you put him straight into the back of the Land Cruiser?" Frank instructed. "It'll transport him directly to the airstrip."

Rose watched as Mayur was driven away. The Amref plane would collect him and transport him to the Aga Khan Hospital in Nairobi.

CHAPTER TWENTY-THREE

Mr Butler looked across at Jono, who was slumped in the corner of the guard post tent with his back to the group.

Marina suggested, "I'll ask Mama Rose and Chloe to keep an eye on him."

Thabiti trailed out of the tent behind Mr Butler and his teammates. What had caused the winch to break? He'd tested it with Mr Obado on a small slope outside Nanyuki and it had worked perfectly. So what had happened today?

Had he forgotten to tighten something? His mind spun and he couldn't think straight. All he could see was the car rolling over down the hill and Mayur hanging upside down in the driver's seat. He felt his chin quiver.

Sam joined him. "Don't go tormenting yourself. We have to work out what happened before we can even think about apportioning blame." Sam placed an arm around him and manoeuvred him over to the crash site.

Thabiti hung back as the team crowded around the car and Mr Butler began his investigation. After walking around the car, taking notes on a clipboard, he found the winch cable, followed it to its end, and picked up the D-Ring. "Who was in charge of this winch?"

"I was." Sam stepped forward. "That D-ring was attached to the winch strop which I had secured around two trees at the top of the slope."

"We'd better take a look up there then." Mr Butler and Sam clambered up the slope followed by Marina and Thabiti. George remained with the car.

Marina shivered despite the midday heat. "If Mama Rose hadn't shouted, and George hadn't quickly pulled me out of the way, I would have been squashed under the car."

"I was lucky not to be lashed by the winch cable as it spun past me. If the D-ring is still attached, it means the strop or the supporting trees broke," murmured Thabiti.

At the top of the slope they stood aside as Car 48 approached. "Is that your car?" a breathless runner in a yellow t-shirt asked as he peered down the slope.

Thabiti shuffled backwards, looked back down the slope, and heard Marina answer, "Yes, it looks terrible from up here, doesn't it? But don't worry, there's nobody in it now. We managed to get our driver out and he's being flown to Nairobi. I'm afraid we don't know how badly injured he is."

"Gosh, what happened?" the man asked.

"I'm not exactly sure. That's what Mr Butler is trying to find out. I think it was something to do with the winch."

"You can't use these trees to secure your winch." Thabiti looked up as Mr Butler turned away another yellow-shirted team member. "At least not until I've finished my accident assessment."

Car 48 found another anchor point and Marina and Thabiti dodged out of its way as it proceeded down the hill without incident.

They approached Mr Butler who commented, "There's

nothing wrong with these trees. In fact, they make an excellent anchor point."

Thabiti wandered away, scuffing the ground. He glimpsed something yellow and spotted the winch strop dangling from a leleshwa bush. As he pulled it out, the cause of the accident was obvious. One of the loops at the end was broken and its protective nylon sleeve lay on the floor. "Over here," he called unenthusiastically.

Mr Butler examined the offending strop. "It's clear that the stitching has given way." He looked up. "Do we know when this was last tested?"

Everyone looked at Thabiti.

"Last week, in Nanyuki," he muttered. He felt his throat constricting, but he added, "Mr Obado and I used it to practice winching the car."

"May I?" Sam stretched out his arm. He examined the broken loop and took photos with his phone.

Mr Butler said, "I know Mr Obado, so I'll speak to him about the accident and the winch strop. Now, I'd better be getting back, in case there are more crises. Would anyone like a lift to headquarters?"

"I'll stay with the car," replied Sam.

"So will I." Thabiti felt an ache at the bottom of his stomach. He couldn't face returning to headquarters just yet.

"Someone really ought to be with Lavi and Kumar," said Marina. Nobody responded. "Ok, I'll go back. Can I have a lift?" she asked Mr Butler. "And I think we should take Jono with us, and ask the medics at headquarters to check him over. He's not in a good way."

Before he got into his car, Mr Butler turned to Thabiti and Sam. "There may be a formal investigation." He looked directly at Thabiti. "I'm not sure if we have to report the incident to the police. It may depend on how badly injured your driver is."

Thabiti felt his heartbeat accelerate. Surely it was an accident. The winch strop had been fine when he last checked. He wasn't to blame for what happened. He prayed Mayur would make a speedy recovery.

CHAPTER TWENTY-FOUR

Pearl placed the blue yoga mat that her instructor had lent her on the grass at the back of the class. There were seven other participants, six women and a man, who were at least sixty and lived in the residential care annex attached to the hospital.

Their instructor, Ajay, was an Indian man, which had surprised Pearl. She had expected a lycra-clad forty-something mzungu with long hair tied back in a ponytail.

Ajay welcomed the group. He put his hands together, bowed, and said, "Namaste". The elderly women chorused "Namaste" and bowed as one, smiling back. Pearl felt her skin tighten and she looked away. These grey-haired ladies had a crush on their instructor. She returned her focus to the front and found Ajay staring expectantly at her. She sighed, bowed and mumbled, "Namaste".

Maybe she had made a mistake returning to the class this afternoon, but after yesterday's session she had felt calmer, and she'd had the best night's sleep in ages. Her jumbled thoughts had returned this morning, but they were less persistent than normal.

Ajay played soothing music from his phone and

instructed, "Down Dog". Pearl lowered her hands to the floor and pushed her bum up and backwards, straightening her legs. The lady in front farted, and Pearl collapsed onto her hands and knees giggling.

"Again," Ajay instructed the class. She felt his presence. "Push down into your heels, Pearl. Well done."

When it came to the balance routine, the group was all over the place. The man found a wall and rested one hand against it for stability. Most of the women were like Pearl, swaying precariously on one leg until they dropped their foot to the floor to steady themselves. An ancient-looking lady at the front balanced serenely on one leg, whilst her other foot rested on her knee, mimicking a flamingo. Well, if she can do it, so can I, thought Pearl. She raised her left leg.

She managed to rest her foot above her ankle. She brought her hands together and focused on the peak of Mount Kenya, just visible through a break in the cloud. "Good, Pearl. Squeeze your core muscles and ground yourself through your right leg."

She enjoyed the meditation section at the end of the class and allowed her mind to drift as her muscles relaxed.

Ajay approached her as she rolled up her mat. "Well done. You're learning quickly." He handed her a leaflet. "I'm running a retreat at a new lodge in Borana next month. It's a small, select group and, as well as yoga, there is a spa, bush walks and plenty of time to relax."

"Thanks," she responded automatically. A yoga retreat. She could barely think of a worse way to spend her time, all those hippy types.

"It's a young crowd and no hippy types." Had he read her mind? She was still standing in a daze when a voice called her name.

"Pearl." She turned and found Mr Kariuki watching her. Well, he couldn't actually see her, but it was rather spooky.

"Join me." He patted the empty space beside him on the bench. "Give me your hand."

Gingerly, she allowed him to take her hand and turn it over. He ran a finger over her wrist and palm. "Ah, your spirit is strengthening and your demons retreating. You will continue with this yoga?"

"I'm not sure," she responded. She wasn't going to commit to anything in front of this old man.

"You will," he nodded. "As your body strengthens so will your mind, and you'll embrace the power and energy you will begin to feel. But what then?"

"Yoga's enough at the moment." Pearl extracted her hand.

"You should consider Ju-jitsu. Not the pure Japanese martial art, but a slightly different version called Zujitsu which was developed by a brother of colour in America. It blends self-defence with street-fighting moves and incorporates dance and fighting rhythms." He took her hand again and placed her palm against his. "You have the warrior spirit. I feel it."

CHAPTER TWENTY-FIVE

At six o'clock, after a tiring day, Rose returned to the Rhino Charge Headquarters. It was alive and buzzing as supporters and spectators congratulated, or commiserated, with competitors. Cars in various states of disrepair were parked in parc fermé.

Rose thought she spotted the doorless blue side of Car 27. Thabiti and Sam had helped retrieve it when a recovery vehicle arrived at the guard post, and accompanied it back to base.

"I need a shower and some peace and quiet," Rose told Chloe.

"Good idea," said Chloe, but as they passed the bar tent, a member of a celebrating team grabbed Chloe by the waist, spun her around, and thrust a glass of champagne into her hand. Chloe laughed, waved at Rose, and joined the group.

Rose was relieved to finally be by herself. She appreciated Chloe's company, but knew the girl needed some fun and a reprieve from her own troubles. She was worried about Chloe's home life. Dan was away a lot, but things seemed worse when he was home.

And poor Kumar. Rose wondered if he or Lavanya had

accompanied Mayur in the plane to Nairobi. She'd find out after she'd taken a shower.

"Rose." She turned to see Tanya West hurrying towards her. "Rose, we've a small problem." Rose waited for her to explain. "One of the teams brought back a baby oryx."

"Did they? But what about its mother? Where is she?" Rose asked.

"They said she wasn't around. I do hope they didn't scare her away."

Reluctantly, Rose retraced her steps, past the lively bar, to the registration tent. At the back, curled up in a cardboard box, was the rich chestnut-brown coated baby oryx. Thankfully, it lacked the long straight ridged horns that an adult developed. As Rose knelt down, it lifted its head, showing forlorn sunken eyes. She gently pulled the skin on the animal's neck, which remained sticking out rather than springing back into place.

"How is the wee thing?" Wendy Butler leaned over the box.

"Frightened and dehydrated. It can't stay here with all this noise."

Wendy sighed. "I agree. When I get a chance, I'll call around the lodges and see if one of them will take it. But they probably won't collect it until tomorrow, as all the vehicles will be out with guests on evening game drives."

Rose hesitated. She didn't want the responsibility of a baby oryx at the moment, although she was happy to provide any care and medical attention it needed.

Perhaps Wendy correctly interpreted her silence. "We'll keep it in our tent overnight until someone comes for it. Tell me what we need to do."

"If you have a spare blanket, put it in the box to help keep it warm. Now, I wonder if there is anyone at the Charge with a baby, who would be willing to give us a spare baby bottle with a teat. I really need to get it to drink some water and electrolytes in the next few hours."

Wendy became business-like. "You've had a long day out at your guard post and you must be feeling pretty grubby. Why don't you have a shower, and I'll get someone to take the oryx to our tent? And I'll ask around for a baby bottle so you can feed it back at our camp, where it will be quieter."

Rose reached the officials camp without further interruptions. "Can you prepare water for a shower?" she asked the stained white-shirted member of camp staff. Water was already being heated in a large oil drum over a wood fire. He tipped some hot water into a white container, carried it over to one of the canvas-clad shower cubicles, and hoisted it aloft.

A pipe dropped down from the container with a shower head attached to its end. Rose entered the cubicle and when she was ready, she reached up, turned a lever in the pipe, and water sprayed out. She relaxed as water ran over her wrinkled body and she felt some of the day's tension wash away.

She dressed in a pair of jeans, a clean striped shirt, and draped a fleece jacket around her shoulders.

"Mama Rose, Memsahib Wendy brought the baby animal and ask me to give you this." The man handed her a small plastic baby bottle. "It in that tent." He pointed across at another green canvas tent whose front flap was tied open.

Rose returned to her own tent, opened a bottle of water, and poured some into the baby bottle. In a side pocket of her canvas bag she found a clear plastic bag with various packets inside, including a natural-flavoured rehydration sachet containing electrolytes and glucose. She tipped the powder into the bottle, screwed on the teat top, and shook it to mix the solution. Now all she had to do was persuade the young oryx to drink it.

Rose peered inside Wendy and Frank's tent. The oryx had

been placed in the front corner and was partially covered by a red and green shuka blanket. It appeared calmer and its eyes, although still sunken, did not flash in fear.

"There we go, that's better isn't it? It's much quieter here." Rose's voice was soft and soothing.

She slowly lowered herself and sat down next to the oryx's box. She gently prodded the animal's lips with the teat and although they wrinkled, its mouth didn't open. "Come on, open wide. You need to drink this."

She leaned forward and massaged the oryx's lips with her index finger. They wrinkled again and she reached into the corner of its mouth and inserted the teat. Its head recoiled, but then leant toward her. Rose tried again and this time the small antelope sucked at the teat. It began to drink.

"There's a good little thing," Rose cooed.

CHAPTER TWENTY-SIX

Rose left the baby oryx in peace after it had drunk most of the contents of its bottle. She wanted to find a member of the Amref medical staff so they could provide her with an update on Mayur. She was also concerned about Jono, who had reacted badly to today's accident.

As she approached the medical tent, she heard a man shout. It sounded like Mayur, but surely he was in a Nairobi hospital. Stepping closer, she recognised Mayur's voice as he shouted in Hindi and although she couldn't understand the words, their meaning was clear. Lavanya ran out of the tent, her head bowed as she hastily covered it with a scarf to hide her tear-stained face.

Rose was torn. Should she comfort the poor girl? Her inquisitiveness got the better of her. She wanted to know why Mayur was still here and why he'd bellowed at Lavanya.

"Leave the poor girl alone," another voice yelled. Jono's voice.

"You'd like that wouldn't you? You had your chance, but you abandoned her. Now she's mine."

"I didn't have a choice, but as she is your wife, treat her with some respect."

"Why? You can't make me," Mayur taunted.

Rose didn't want to become entangled in this debate. It was clear that there was no love lost between Mayur and Jono, and Lavanya appeared to be at the bottom of it. She tiptoed away from the tent and followed Lavanya through the leleshwa bushes into the Bandit Bush Hog's camp.

Kumar Chauhan was seated silently at one end of the table in the events shelter. At the other end, Marina and Thabiti had their heads close together, speaking quietly to each other.

"Ah, Rose, please come and join us," called Kumar. "I'm afraid Lakshmi has not smiled favourably on us today." He tapped the ends of his fingers together.

"Please, accept my sympathy." Rose joined him. "And how is Mayur?"

"His injuries include a broken arm and whiplash, and he is very bruised and battered. Actually, he's still here, in the medical tent. And it's very clear the accident hasn't shaken his spirit." Kumar looked at Lavanya as she placed samosas on the table. His eyes softened. Rose noted bruising around Lavanya's wrist.

"Great," cried Thabiti. "I'm starving, as I haven't had a thing to eat all day." He grabbed a samosa and dipped it in a bowl of tomato chutney.

Lavanya sat next to Kumar, but pushed her chair back from the table. She bowed her head and twisted the ends of her scarf. Rose spotted another, older bruise on her neck, partially covered by the scarf.

"Thabiti, please remember, we make a prayer of thanks before we eat." Kumar's stare was cold.

Chastised, Thabiti put the half-eaten samosa on the table and waited.

Kumar said, "You can say your own prayer. You are a

grown man. And you have to account to the gods for your actions."

Thabiti blinked rapidly before he closed his eyes, mumbled something, and picked up the remains of the samosa.

"So why is Mayur still here?" Rose asked. "I expected him to be in Nairobi."

"There was an issue with the Amref planes, and the one that should have flown here was called away to Impala Ranch, in Laikipia, to airlift a casualty. But the medics have patched him up and he seems comfortable enough. We will leave with him in the morning."

Kumar glanced towards the entrance and frowned as Sam strode towards them. "Here comes your partner in crime, Thabiti." He turned to Lavanya and spoke quietly. "My dear, can you help me up?"

Sam sat down opposite Rose and tossed his phone on the table.

"Are you OK?" Rose inquired. "What have you been doing?"

"Checking up on things." Sam clasped his hands together. "I took another look at the winch strop." He grabbed his phone. "See this."

Sam passed the phone across, and she peered at a photo of a yellow strip of webbing. "What am I looking for?" she asked.

"The stitching." Sam took his phone, enlarged the photo and swivelled it back to her. "Can you see those loose threads? They held the ends of the winch strop together to form a loop. And although some of them are frayed, from being torn apart, other threads have clean ends as if they've been cut.

So I think someone deliberately tampered with the strop, by cutting a few strands. And then they concealed the damage

94

by covering the join with the strop's sleeve. As the pressure on the strop increased, the stitching ripped until it gave way."

"Are you saying this wasn't an accident?" asked Rose. "That the strop was deliberately tampered with?"

"Yes, I am." Sam sat back and crossed his arms.

"But not by me," cried Thabiti. "I know everyone thinks it's my fault. Just look at the way Mr Kumar spoke to me this evening."

"You know he doesn't like anyone eating without saying a prayer," chided Marina.

"It wasn't just that. There were other comments as well. Now I think he regrets allowing Sam and me to join the team."

"He's bound to be upset," comforted Rose. "He probably feels guilty he wasn't the one driving. Remember, his son is badly injured and the car will cost a fortune to repair. Who knows if he will carry on with the Rhino Charge after this."

"Anyway, back to the car." Sam drummed his fingers on the table. "Did Thabiti tell you someone already sabotaged it and tried to stop the team taking part?"

"No!" cried Rose and Marina in unison.

"You show them," Sam told Thabiti.

"Those are the electronic connectors for the starter plugs in the engine." Thabiti enlarged an image on his phone. "When they're disconnected like that, the engine won't start. But they have their own covering, so I didn't notice the problem when I first looked."

Rose asked, "But who would deliberately interfere with the Bandit Bush Hog's car?"

CHAPTER TWENTY-SEVEN

Rose woke early on Tuesday morning. Around her, the camp was quiet apart from the muted voices of camp staff preparing hot water for showers and early morning drinks. A car from one of the safari lodges had collected the baby oryx the previous evening, which had saved her and Wendy from having to get up in the night to feed it. Rose hoped the lonely young animal would survive.

She decided to stretch her legs with a walk through the headquarters whilst it was still calm, and unconsciously she arrived at the medical tent. Should she check on Jono, and Mayur before he was airlifted to Nairobi?

The zip was undone, so she tentatively pulled aside the white entrance flap and peered inside. Only one bed was occupied. That meant Jono must have left the previous evening. It was deathly still. She was about to leave, as she didn't want to wake Mayur, but something caused her to turn back.

The bed Jono had occupied was dishevelled and his pillow lay across rumpled sheets. Mayur's top sheet was also untucked, and it did not fully cover him. As she tiptoed inside, she noted his left arm was supported by a cotton sling, but the bruised forearm was free and lay across his hip. She paused and sniffed the air.

There was a stale stillness, and she shivered, feeling a spirit fill the air and disperse. Had that been Mayur's soul? She knew from his lifeless, bloodshot eyes and the pale sheen of his skin that he was dead.

She'd only just met Mayur, and thoroughly disapproved of his treatment of Lavanya, but yesterday he had been courageous and full of determination. Her Catholic faith was strong, but she still found it hard to accept the death of younger, healthy people.

How long had Mayur been dead, and had he suffered? She glanced once more at his body and noted a bruise on the top of his exposed hip. Had he died from internal bleeding as a result of trauma from the car accident? Would Thabiti be blamed for Mayur's death? The officials thought him responsible for the damaged winch strop, which had caused the car to roll and, by doing so, injure Mayur.

Rose turned and stepped over a blanket, which had fallen to the floor. It covered a blue piece of plastic, and there were puddles of water, from an upturned glass, beside the second bed. She left quietly. Mayur had not looked peaceful and Rose imagined him fighting his death.

Rose returned to the medical tent with Nick West, the Rhino Charge organiser, and a paramedic from Amref. The headquarters was starting to come to life and she could smell coffee and bacon. Her stomach rumbled.

"Rose, have you told anyone else about this?" Nick asked.

"No, I thought it best to come straight to you."

The paramedic pulled the sheet back to Mayur's waist: he still wore his blue team t-shirt. "I can confirm he is dead,"

said the paramedic, straightening up. "But not when he died."
Nick remained at the end of the bed, averting his gaze from
the body.

Rose moved to the paramedic's side. "Do you have any
idea what caused it?"

"My guess is internal haemorrhaging. Was he the one
extracted from a car which rolled yesterday?"

"Yes, he was, and I witnessed the accident. It was rather
frightening as the car flipped over from a height of several
metres."

"But it was fitted with a safety cage, and he was strapped
into a harness and wore a helmet," Nick said, but leaned away
from the bed.

"Even so, that type of accident would assert a lot of
pressure on the body. My colleague, who examined him
yesterday, may not have known about the internal damage."
The paramedic rolled Mayur's body over and lifted his shirt.
"Look, there is dark bruising along his spine where blood has
settled."

"This is a catastrophe for the Rhino Charge." Nick
chewed the end of pen. "The authorities may use it as an
excuse to cancel future events."

The paramedic lifted the bed sheet and laid it across
Mayur, covering his body and face. "Then you need to have
him examined by the Nairobi medical officer, but he is a busy
man and spends most of his time in court. I would
recommend contacting him before involving the police."

CHAPTER TWENTY-EIGHT

Outside the medical tent, Nick turned to Rose. "I need to inform Mayur's next of kin. I know his father, Kumar, but I wonder if there is anyone else I should speak to."

"There's his wife, a timid lady called Lavanya." Rose gazed up at the clear blue sky. Too beautiful a day to be giving such painful news.

"Do you know them?" Nick inquired.

"A little, and I've spent some time in their camp this week as my young friend Thabiti is their team's mechanic." Rose noted Nick's lip curl. "Would you like me to come with you?"

Nick's shoulders relaxed. "Yes, please."

The Bandit Bush Hog's camp was a hive of activity as bed rolls and bags lay outside partially dismantled tents.

Kumar sat alone in the events shelter. He spotted Nick and asked, "Is the plane here? We're almost ready to leave. I'm sending the bags and equipment back to Nairobi by car." He saw Rose and added curtly, "If you're looking for Thabiti, he left with Sam."

Rose did not respond and looked at Nick as they sat down at the table.

Lavanya appeared. "Would you like a drink?" she asked.

"Not at the moment, dear," answered Rose. "Would you mind sitting down?"

Lavanya looked across at Kumar who nodded his consent.

Kumar leant forward. "Something's happened? What is it? Is it Mayur?" His voice rose with each question.

Rose looked at Nick again who opened his mouth but no words emerged.

She squeezed her hands into fists, exhaled and said, "I'm so very sorry. Mayur died during the night. I found him in the medical tent this morning."

Lavanya cried out. She covered her face with her hand and turned away.

Kumar held Rose's gaze and his facial muscles tightened, but his voice remained steady. "How? I know he had some serious injuries, including a broken arm, but he was lucid and conscious yesterday. He was certainly well enough to upset Lavanya when she took him some supper."

Kumar's hands began to shake. Rose touched his arm. "We believe yesterday's accident caused some internal damage and bleeding which nobody was aware of. But we can't be certain without a formal examination, or autopsy."

"But how can you do that out here?" Kumar's voice began to crack.

Nick finally found his own voice. "I'd like to fly in the Nairobi medical officer, but I understand he's a difficult man to pin down."

"I know him, so let me make a call. On the practical side, do you have anywhere cool to…" Kumar's voice became hoarse and he swallowed, "store my son's body?"

Nick shook his head.

Lavanya ran from the table. Kumar sat up straight. "Now

please leave me. I will let you know about the medical officer when I have an answer."

At the camp entrance Rose met Thabiti and Marina. She looked back at Kumar. His quiet dignity had shattered as he sat hunched over the table, his whole body wracked with the sobs Rose could feel rather than hear.

"Thank you for your help, Rose," Nick said and walked away in the direction of the registration tent.

Marina tugged at her t-shirt. "We've just heard a rumour that Mayur's dead."

Rose closed her eyes and shook her head. "Now that's quick even by Kenyan standards. We've only just told Kumar and Lavanya."

"So it's true." Thabiti's voice was dull and he kicked a stone with his foot.

"Marina," a man's voice called. "Baba's looking for you." One of the young men Rose had seen in Deepak Seth's Rhino Charge team ran towards them. "He's heard about Mayur's death."

"I know. I've just heard. It's terrible, but what does Baba want?"

"You away from criminals," shouted Marina's father as he arrived at the camp entrance.

"Baba, what criminals?"

"Him." The old man poked Thabiti in the chest with surprising strength. Thabiti staggered backwards, his eyes wide with surprise.

"Baba, stop. Thabiti isn't a criminal."

"I heard Mayur Chauhan is dead. And that he died of his injuries from yesterday's crash. A crash caused by his ineptitude." Marina's father stared at Thabiti who flinched and stepped further back. "You're coming with us."

Marina protested, "But Baba…"

She was cut off by her father, who snapped, "Don't argue.

That team - your team - has a habit of killing people in car accidents, as you well know."

With her elderly father on one side and the young man on the other, Marina was frogmarched away. She turned her head and looked back at Thabiti, her eyes wide with despair.

"They can't do that," exclaimed Thabiti.

"They just did," replied Rose. She gazed into the distance and was not aware she spoke out loud. "What did he mean by 'your team has a habit of killing people in car accidents'?"

"I've no idea." Thabiti moaned. "But we need to see Sam."

CHAPTER TWENTY-NINE

Rose felt a static charge in the air as she and Thabiti walked through the headquarters. People eyed Thabiti surreptitiously and began whispering to their companions.

Thabiti must have noticed as well, as he scuffed his feet along the ground and shoved his hands into his pockets. Sam approached them and glowered at anyone who glanced in Thabiti's direction. "I'm sorry you have to put up with this, Thabiti. We need to find out what happened, and quickly, before all these people judge you as guilty."

Rose followed Sam into the parc fermé to the doorless blue Car 27. He was once again covered in dust. "I've checked every inch of this vehicle."

Sam ran his hand across the side of the car. "And I found a nail in one of the spare tyres, an empty diesel canister, and the remote control for the front winch doesn't work. Now the crash may have damaged the remote control, but it didn't put a nail in the spare wheel or empty the fuel canister."

Rose walked to the front of the car. "Are you saying this is more evidence to support your sabotage theory?"

"I believe it's more than coincidence, but others might not. Most people already think Thabiti is incompetent, so not checking a spare tyre or forgetting to fill up the spare fuel canister is easy to believe."

Rose tapped the vehicle's bonnet and mused, "But not the interference with the engine."

"I'm not sure it's enough. It's just one incident amongst many." Sam's arms hung by his sides.

"But you said the stitching on the winch strop was cut?" Rose covered her eyes from the sun as she watched Sam.

"I believe it was, but it's very hard to prove. There are lots of little things that a nervous, inexperienced mechanic might have overlooked."

Rose and Sam focused on Thabiti, who raised his arms in the air. "So what do I do?"

Rose walked back to them, thinking through the problem. "We need to find out who did interfere with the car. Do you remember? Mayur accused Deepak Seth of causing issues in Nairobi which prevented Mayur's brother and teammate joining the Charge. Do you think Deepak would go as far as deliberately damaging your car?"

Sam replied, "I doubt so personally, but there are plenty of younger men on his team."

Thabiti spoke. "When?"

"When what?" queried Rose.

"When could any of Deepak's team sabotage this car? It was transported directly from Nanyuki and parked in the middle of our camp. Yesterday night, before the Charge, it was securely left in here."

Rose patted the car. "I'm sure there were times when the camp was empty."

"Once, and that was only for ten minutes," explained Thabiti. "When we registered the team. During the briefings Lavanya remained behind."

Rose looked around parc fermé. The cars were parked haphazardly in various states of disrepair. One had a smashed windscreen, another was held up by a jack, its wheel missing, whilst a blue car next to them looked as if it had not even competed.

Sam walked across to the plastic mesh fence. "I know this enclosure is named after the secure compound at Formula One races, but it's easy enough to climb over this fence, and we all know night askaris are prone to sleeping on the job."

"So you're saying someone could have entered this compound and caused the damage," concluded Rose.

Thabiti trudged round to the back of the car. "Not to the engine, and not to the winch strop, which was locked in this metal box in the back. And only Kumar has the key."

Rose held her hands up in surrender. "My head's swimming. What I need is a refreshing cup of tea."

They wandered along to the Dormans coffee stand and found Chloe seated at one of the tables. She was leaning back in her chair with large sunglasses covering her eyes. Rose expected Thabiti to make a joke, but he remained silent and brooding.

"Chloe, are you sleeping?" Rose demanded, peering down at her.

Chloe started in her chair and sat up slowly. "Aw, my head's sore. Please don't shout."

Sam grinned, "Ah, you had a late night celebrating?"

"It's all right for some," Thabiti mumbled under his breath and turned away.

Chloe removed her glasses, displaying pink-tinged eyes. "Who got out of bed on the wrong side this morning?"

"Well, at least he got out," quipped Rose. "Sorry, I didn't mean to snap. Have you heard on the jungle drums that Mayur Chauhan is dead?"

Clearly Chloe had not, as her mouth formed a large 'O'. "Sit down whilst I buy everyone drinks and then you can tell me all about it."

While they waited, Rose described how she found the body.

Chloe tapped her foot. "Why didn't someone check on him during the night?"

"Your drinks are ready," one of the Dormans staff shouted.

Sam jumped up. "I'll get them."

"I guess," said Rose, "that nobody wanted to disturb him and thought that letting him sleep would be the best cure."

Chloe persisted, "But surely he would have cried out in pain?"

Rose took her tea from Sam, who had already added milk and removed the tea bag. She took a grateful sip of the hot liquid. "Not necessarily. We know the headquarters was noisy last night and the medical staff probably joined in the fun. They'd worked hard helping at guard posts as well as treating injuries.

Anyway, if Mayur died of internal bleeding, as we think he did, the loss of blood would have caused him to slip into unconsciousness before he passed away. His painkillers might have helped mask his pain."

The group was sombre and silent as they drank. Rose thought of it as a toast to the departed Mayur.

Thabiti glanced at his companions and looked down. "I wonder when Jono left the medical tent? I saw him this morning emerging from his tent in camp and chatting to Lavi. I didn't sleep very well last night, probably because I was worrying about the accident, and it was very noisy. Lots of people seemed to be up late." He squinted in Chloe's direction. "So I'm not sure when Jono returned."

"Then we should ask him," stated Rose. "But first we all need breakfast as it could be another long day."

CHAPTER THIRTY

M any competitors and supporters had also decided to
have breakfast at the Rusty Nail in the centre of
headquarters, including Jono who sat alone, hunched over a
table, away from the main crowd. Rose hesitated, considering
it might be too intimidating if Sam, Thabiti, Chloe, and
herself all descended on him.

Chloe must have noticed. "I'll cheer up Thabiti and leave
you and Sam to chat with Jono." She pulled a protesting
Thabiti into the breakfast queue and thrust a paper menu into
his hand. Rose heard her say, "I'm starving. What do you
want?"

Sam nudged Rose. "Go and sit with Jono. I'll order for us
both, and then join you. Is an egg and bacon roll OK?"

Rose kept her eyes on Jono as she answered, "That
sounds great. I have a tab open so put the order on that."
Weaving between tables, Rose pulled out a chair and sat
down next to Jono.

He stared at his untouched breakfast roll, twirling his
penknife in his fingers. "Mayur's dead."

"I know," replied Rose. "I was the one who found him."

He looked at her with hollow eyes and a haunted

expression. "Was he dead when I left... or did I leave him to die?"

"I don't know," Rose responded. "Tell me what happened last night. Why didn't you sleep in the medical tent?"

"Mayur had been in a foul mood all afternoon. Then Lavi brought us both some chapatis and hot lentil soup. I was really grateful as I hadn't eaten all day and the soup was delicious. But instead of being appreciative, Mayur shouted at her and she ran away. I was furious with Mayur, but he told me to go to hell, so I left him alone and returned to camp."

Sam placed two egg and bacon rolls on the table and sat down. He and Jono exchanged nodded greetings.

Rose pulled her plate towards her and asked Jono, "Do you know what time it was when you got back?"

"I think around half past nine. The bar was busy, but our camp was quiet and I didn't see anyone."

Sam bit into his roll and used a napkin to remove the egg yolk which ran down his chin.

Jono mirrored his action and bit into his roll.

Rose did the same, considering Jono. On the plane journey to the Mara he had appeared relaxed, jovial, and carefree, but ever since they entered headquarters, his manner had changed. He was withdrawn, even morose. Something was troubling him, and Mayur's death had not improved his disposition.

She looked across at Chloe and Thabiti, who were both concentrating on eating. Thabiti was her priority at the moment. She had to clear him of the accusations that he'd neglected his mechanic's duties.

She placed her partially eaten roll back on the plate. "Jono, Sam is concerned that someone tampered with your team's car."

Jono's eyes narrowed. "By doing what?"

Sam wiped his mouth and answered. "Mostly small things

like a nail in the spare tyre and emptying one of the spare fuel cans. But before scrutineering, someone interfered with the engine, and of course, someone cut the stitching on the winch strop."

Jono gulped and dropped his sandwich. "But I thought the officials said it was an accident. And that Thabiti hadn't taken the care to check it."

Sam finished his sandwich and sat back. "I know they did, but I disagree with them."

Rose leaned forward and said conspiratorially, "We think someone else, possibly a member of Deepak Seth's team, deliberately interfered with your team's car to prevent you taking part. I doubt they intended to injure or kill anyone, but just wanted to stop you finishing." She paused and looked intently at Jono who leaned back. "Do you have any idea who could have done this and why?"

Jono clenched his hands together, hesitating. In a tense voice he said, "I know there's no love lost between Kumar and Deepak Seth. It's got something to do with business and happened many years ago. Kumar told me Deepak is so obsessed with beating his team at the Rhino Charge that they usually push themselves too far and fail to finish or wreck their car. I think Rhino Force have only beaten the Bandit Bush Hogs once."

Colour returned to Jono's cheeks and he ate another mouthful of his breakfast. He swallowed and added, "Kumar is generous and gives people a chance. That's why he accepted my suggestion that Thabiti join the team, and you saw how he overruled Mayur and allowed Marina to take part."

Jono was into his stride. "That really annoyed Mayur. You see, he resented his father who is successful, generous, and well liked. You heard how he wanted to move and modernise the business, but Kumar refused to consider his plans.

Besides, Kumar still runs the business, which Mayur also resented."

Rose decided it was time to steer the discussion back to possible candidates for sabotaging the car. "But what about the relationship between Kumar and Deepak? Could it have caused enough resentment for Deepak to resort to underhand means to beat Kumar's team? And if he didn't actually damage the car himself, could he have persuaded someone else to do it for him?"

Jono cocked his head to one side. "I really don't think Kumar was bothered by Deepak, although he might have been amused. I've watched him this weekend greet Deepak and laugh when he only receives a grunted response."

Jono's brow furrowed. "I don't know Deepak that well, but he comes across as a bitter old man. So could he have persuaded someone to tamper with our car? Yes, he could." Jono looked down at his partly eaten roll and pushed his plate away. Rose realised he was sinking back into his own troubled world.

"Thank you for your help." She collected her half-eaten roll and rejoined Chloe and Thabiti.

Chloe looked across at Jono. "He doesn't look as if he was much help."

Rose sat down and said, "Well, he admitted Deepak Seth is desperate to beat the Bandit Bush Hogs, and his grudge against Kumar is large enough that he could have instructed someone to sabotage the team's car. But we're no nearer to finding out who." She finished her breakfast and pondered her next move.

Sitting up, she tapped the table with both hands and announced. "I need to find Marina and get to the bottom of what happened to her Uncle Deepak, and why he's so bitter."

CHAPTER THIRTY-ONE

Rose stood under the gazebo at the entrance to Deepak Seth's Rhino Force team camp. Marina's bossy cousin, Elaxi, the plump woman who had wanted Marina to entertain her children on Saturday evening, demanded, "Can I help you?"

"I'm just looking for Marina." Rose cast her gaze around the camp.

Elaxi stood with her hands on her thighs, blocking Rose's way, and asked, "Are you one of those Bandit Bush Hog's supporters?"

Rose crossed her fingers. "I'm an official." She wasn't telling a lie and she felt guilty about the deception, but it was important to find and speak to Marina. She was certain that whatever troubled her Uncle Deepak was at the bottom of his feud with Kumar, and possibly the sabotage of the Bandit Bush Hog's team car.

Elaxi suspiciously pointed Rose towards Marina, who was sitting outside a small blue tent reading a book. As Rose approached, Marina looked up and asked, "How is Thabiti?"

Rose pressed a finger to her lips. "I told your cousin Elaxi that I was an official. I'm sorry to disturb your reading, but

I'd like to chat with you." Rose watched a group of men, including members of the Rhino Force team, play cricket with some children, encouraged by older men and women who stood or sat watching the game.

"Shall we go somewhere quieter and more private?" Rose asked.

Marina hesitated. "I'm not supposed to leave our camp. At least not until Baba calms down and lets me."

"And do you always do as he tells you?"

Marina put the book down and looked up at Rose as she said, "I know I'm twenty-two and act as if I'm independent, but my relief work doesn't give me enough to live on, not in Nairobi anyway. So I have to tread a fine line and know when not to cross it."

Rose knelt down. "I really do need to talk to you. It's about Thabiti, and I need your help to clear his name."

Marina looked around and sighed. "If you don't mind a bit of a walk, I know a great place. Wait here." She grabbed a bag and crossed to the central marquee where Rose watched her rummaging in a cool box and some baskets. As she returned to Rose, she shouted to her mother, "I'm going for a walk."

"I'm not sure your father..." Marina strode out of the camp without letting her mother finish.

Both women were silent as Marina confidently led Rose on a path around team camps to the perimeter fence. She held the plastic mesh fence down as Rose clambered over.

"It's not too far now," Marina promised and set off again.

They trekked up a sparsely vegetated slope, scrambling the final few metres onto a large rock. They walked along it, stepping over cracks onto adjacent rocks, until Marina pushed her way through some bushes and they emerged onto a rocky escarpment overlooking the far-reaching Mara plain. Rose drew in her breath. It was such a contrast with the busy camp they'd recently left.

"How did you find this place?" she asked.

"I spoke with the local askaris and asked if there was somewhere quiet with a good view, and they told me how to get here. I wanted to bring Thabiti, but he's too preoccupied at the moment. I can't say I blame him, although I'm not sure I'd want to hang around in camp, not with everyone whispering behind my back, thinking I caused the accident which killed Mayur." Marina sat down and dangled her legs over the edge of the rock.

"Is that the Mara River?" Rose sat beside Marina.

"Yes, meandering its way through the reserve to join with the River Talek. You can spot clumps of tents and the buildings of various lodges from up here."

"It's very brown. I know there hasn't been rain for several weeks, but I don't remember it like this. And where is all the game?" Rose asked.

Marina swung her legs and replied, "It's such a shame. I've done relief work at some of the Mara lodges and they are very worried about the future."

Rose turned towards Marina. "Are they under pressure from the people living on the edge of the reserve?"

"Exactly. There's a growing population which sees this great expanse of land kept aside for wildlife and foreign tourists. It's understandable they want a part of it. But the problem is thousands of cattle are spilling into the Mara each night, and although it's illegal, nobody's stopping them. That's why the ground's so brown. It's mostly sand, as the grass has been lost to over-grazing by cattle. And the sad result of that is the wildlife is now leaving."

Rose continued her search, but couldn't spot the usual herds of zebra or impala. "Did I read something about the

Marsh Pride, which became famous after a UK TV documentary, Big Cat Diaries?"

Marina leaned back and stuck her legs out into space. "What a disaster. The pride has split up as the two stars of the show, Sienna and Bibi, were killed by Maasai herdsmen. They laced a cow carcass with poison in retaliation for the pride killing three cattle. Because of that TV series, tourists come specifically to see the pride.

And I have to explain that we can't control our own people and we've allowed them to illegally kill the very animals they've travelled so far to see. Is it any different from poaching for ivory?"

Rose tilted her head from one side to the other and said, "Remember, the Maasai lifestyle and economy is based around cattle."

"It was based around cattle," Marina corrected. "But if the tribes actually consider where their wealth is coming from now, it's not cattle. They earn a fortune from the conservancy fees visitors pay to visit the Mara. And then there are those tribespeople who earn a living directly from tourists. Many work in the numerous safari camps, and there are village tours and tribal dancing, and some women make beaded necklaces and bracelets which they sell direct to visitors."

Rose chewed her thumb. "It does seem rather short-sighted. And what a tragedy if we lose this iconic reserve. I remember when Craig and I first visited in the early 1970s. The Grammaticas were setting up their first camp. They spent each weekend here with a team clearing vegetation and setting up tents for visitors.

We joined them one weekend and it was magical beside the Mara River. And the vast green plains were teeming with wildlife. Mind you, even back then there were tribal battles over cattle between the Maasai and Kipsigis."

"Do you miss Craig?" Marina asked.

"I do, and I miss those times when everything was an adventure. It seemed so much easier, and we could travel where we wanted and people were happy to see us. I find travelling so much harder now, and dangerous, with crazy drivers and an ever-increasing number of police roadblocks. Also, prices have risen and everything is so expensive. One of the reasons we've enjoyed helping with events such as the Rhino Charge is that we get to visit new, and old places. We couldn't afford to stay in the Mara now."

Pulling herself back to the present Rose knew it was time to forget the view and the fate of the Maasai Mara and tackle the immediate problem of Thabiti.

CHAPTER THIRTY-TWO

Marina removed two bottles of water from her bag and opened a packet of Oreo biscuits, which she offered to Rose.

Rose twisted a black biscuit disc in her fingers and said, "Your family is hiding a secret which I believe is causing Thabiti a great deal of trouble."

Marina choked. She swiftly opened her water bottle and washed down the biscuit. "What do you mean?"

"Well," she said, "you told me a family tragedy triggered Kumar's departure from your Uncle Deepak's business which, if it didn't create an actual feud, initiated a deep-seated animosity between them. Then your father shouted that the Bandit Bush Hogs were a team who 'had a habit of killing people in car accidents'."

"Baba, had no right to say that. Uncle Deepak would be furious."

"Why?" she turned to Marina. "What are you hiding?"

Marina took another drink of water and replied, "If you really want to know, you'd better hear the whole story."

Rose ate her biscuit expectantly.

"They were all at school together in Lavington, in Nairobi," Marina began.

"Who were?"

"My cousins, Uncle Deepak's children. You've met bossy Elaxi in camp. Then there is my oldest cousin, Hinesh, and quieter, bespectacled Aatma. Mayur Chauhan was with them. And Jono Urquhart."

"Jono, in the Bandit Bush Hogs, was at school with Mayur and most of the Rhino Force team?" At last she felt she was getting somewhere.

"He was also friends with cousin Vadhana, Uncle Deepak's youngest daughter, and Mayur's wife, Lavanya." Marina nibbled around the edges of her biscuit.

"Talk about keeping it in the family, and being all the better for burying a secret." Rose knew how secrets could fester and had a habit of bursting forth when least expected, causing renewed pain for those involved. "Am I right?"

Marina ignored her question. "Jono went to college in the UK and quiet cousin Aatma went to Leicester, a British university. My older cousins and their friends were already working."

"So what happened?"

"Cousin Vadhana went to the UK and stayed with Aatma. And they both visited Jono. It was winter and very cold and frosty. Jono was driving too fast down a hill and the car didn't make the turn. The speed limit was thirty miles per hour and the car was travelling at forty-five. The coroner concluded that in normal weather conditions, at that speed, the car would have stayed on the road." Marina stopped. She was shaking and rubbed her hand against her mouth.

"A coroner means someone died. Was it your cousin Vadhana?" Rose laid her arm around Marina's shoulder.

Marina nodded. "She was eighteen. It happened twenty

years ago when I was only a toddler, but the family continue to mourn for her."

"And Jono was responsible for her death?"

Marina swallowed. "He was driving and Vadhana was in the passenger seat. She was killed and Jono was knocked unconscious. Aatma, in the back seat, only suffered minor injuries. Mum told me what happened, but the rest of the family refuse to talk about the accident."

Rose thought of the slumped form of Jono over the breakfast table earlier. "Reuniting Jono with his old school mates, at a driving event, must have reawakened the nightmare of the crash."

Marina sniffed. "I think it's worse than that. The one time I managed to get cousin Aatma to talk, he told me Jono had no memory of the accident. While he was unconscious, he was operated on to remove the swelling on his brain, and he needed six months rehabilitation, by which time Aatma was back in Nairobi."

"Jono has been very self-absorbed and sombre since we arrived at the Rhino Charge. His guilt must be huge and the reason it's taken him twenty years to return to Kenya."

"That and the fact that Uncle Deepak would have killed him. You see, Vadhana was his youngest child and was, as the saying goes, the apple of his eye. He was devastated by her death and it affected everyone around him. Mum said he lashed out at his workers, forgot deliveries, and nearly drove the business to the wall. It was Kumar Chauhan who kept it afloat with the assistance of my cousins. And then there was a huge row and Kumar walked out. After that, the business nearly collapsed, especially when Kumar set up in competition. Uncle Deepak hasn't forgiven him and I don't think my cousins have, either."

That accounted for nearly everyone. "Where was Mayur?"

"He was working in London, and I don't think he joined his father's company for several years. I remember him returning to Kenya and marrying Lavanya. She was at the school on a scholarship and stayed in Nairobi to finish her education. And she was training to be a doctor, but her family decided it was better for her to marry Mayur."

Marina wrinkled her nose. "Can you believe it? She was a bright girl with a promising future in a respectable profession. She could be saving lives now, not tending to the needs of her father-in-law." Her voice was bitter.

"Is that why you were so defensive when you were asked to look after the children in your camp?" Rose opened her water bottle and drank. She was hot sitting on the rock, and the bushes behind her only provided limited shade.

Marina crossed her arms. "I've made it abundantly clear to Baba that he's not finding me a husband. I am quite capable of doing that myself, and I won't be forced into an arranged marriage."

"Does he respect your wishes?"

Her arms dropped to her side. "No, he's completely ignored them. He has 'a nice young man' for me to meet on our return to Nairobi. He's also ordered me to give up my safari work and even threatened to send me back to India to get married if I don't comply."

"Have you talked to anyone about it?" Rose wished she had a hat or sunglasses to shade her eyes from the sun.

"I tried talking to Mama, and she understands, but tells me it's my father's will and I must accept his decision. And there's nobody else I can speak with. Can you believe I have this huge family with aunts, uncles, and cousins, and yet I'm on my own? Even my brother won't go against my father."

"So you have to decide what you want to do."

"I know, but I'm not sure what that is. I hoped the lodge work would provide me with the answers, but it hasn't."

Rose and Marina both stared into the distance without speaking.

Marina broke the silence. "I don't understand why Vadhana's death, twenty years ago, is causing Thabiti problems?"

"Somebody deliberately sabotaged your team's car. It was mostly small things, so I don't believe they actually meant to harm Mayur. No, I think they just wanted to prevent your team taking part, or if you did, stop you from completing the Rhino Charge."

Marina looked down and drew a circle on the rock. "But why now?"

"From what you've told me, Jono is the trigger, and being on Kumar's Bandit Bush Hog team may have rubbed salt into an old wound. I've heard that the Rhino Force team were desperate to beat them and Jono's presence could have provoked one of them to damage your car." Rose prepared herself for the crucial question. "Who do you think is the most likely candidate amongst the Rhino Force team?"

Marina shuffled her bottom. "I really can't believe any of them would do that."

"But if we don't find out who did, it will be Thabiti who takes the blame," countered Rose.

Marina fiddled with her water bottle. "I can't imagine my oldest cousin Hinesh dirtying himself with such work, and I doubt he'd know how. There's the mechanic Uncle Deepak flew in from the UK, but he's a bit straight-laced, so I doubt he'd agree to sabotage another team. My brother might work for Uncle Deepak, but he's not bothered whether they win and just enjoys being part of the team. So that leaves bespectacled cousin Aatma."

"Do you think he would be capable?" Rose probed.

"I don't know. He's clever and very secretive. But I like him, probably because he's also a loner like me, and prefers his own solitude away from the rest of the family. He never puts himself forward and can usually be found reading a book. But he and Uncle Deepak haven't been getting along well for the past few months. I'm not sure why."

"I think we need to find your cousin Aatma."

CHAPTER THIRTY-THREE

S am, Thabiti and Chloe remained at the breakfast table after Rose left.

"I'm worried about Rose," said Chloe. "I know she's just trying to help you, Thabiti, but she could get herself into trouble if she starts asking too many questions."

"Then all the more reason to get to the bottom of this car business and clear Thabiti's name." Sam stood. "Will you excuse us? We have work to do."

Chloe gathered up her bag. "I'm going to lie down for a bit and hope my head stops banging."

"Thabiti," called Sam. "Get up. We need to find Frank Butler."

Thabiti sighed. "Do we have to? I'm sure he'll still blame me."

"Perhaps, but if he formally records my findings we have a better chance of proving your innocence." Sam tugged at Thabiti's t-shirt.

As they left the catering area, Thabiti kept close to Sam, with his head bowed, but he still felt the stares from other competitors. He waited outside the registration tent while Sam entered and asked, "Can I speak with Frank Butler?"

Thabiti kicked at a stone on the ground. He had been so excited about the Rhino Charge and being offered a place as a mechanic. And he'd enjoyed the routine of working at Mr Obado's garage each day, learning how the team's car worked and assisting with other vehicle repairs. Solving a problem with a car, such as a rattling noise or an underperforming engine, gave him a real buzz.

Life was so much better when it had a purpose. He preferred repairing vehicles to drifting about at home or completing crossword puzzles with Craig. That wasn't fair. Craig had helped him develop a routine and given him a reason to get out of bed each day when he really needed one.

Would he return to those lazy mornings, or would he be arrested and thrown into a pit of a prison in Nairobi? What then? Who would look after Pixel? Could he persuade the authorities to move him to Nanyuki jail where his friends could visit him? And what about Pearl? She was still struggling to come to terms with all that happened around Ma's death, and he didn't want her to slide back into her melancholy.

Life had been looking up. He scuffed an image in the sandy ground with his toe. It looked like a wonky heart. He thought of Marina. Was he to be denied her support and companionship? He knew her family were overbearing, but could they actually stop her from seeing him? But would she want to if he was accused and convicted of killing Mayur?

"Thabiti." The voice repeated, "Thabiti." He looked up at Sam, and across at Mr Butler who didn't meet his eyes.

Mr Butler checked his watch. "Can we get on with this? I've loads to do if we're to post the results this afternoon."

Sam led the way to parc fermé and Thabiti trudged along behind. What good would this do? Surely Sam was providing more evidence of his incompetence.

"If this is to be part of the formal investigation, your other team members should be here, particularly your team captain," stated Mr Butler.

"That would hardly be appropriate since we recently lost a team member, and I don't think we should disturb Kumar Chauhan at the moment." Sam's voice had a hard edge. "Jono Urquhart is in a world of his own, and I doubt the runners George and Marina know much about the technicalities of motor vehicles."

Mr Butler's posture was rigid. "There's no need to take that tone." His voice softened. "OK, show me what you've found."

"It's mostly small things. Firstly, there's a nail in one of the spare tyres." Sam reached into the back of the car, dragged a tyre towards him and found the offending nail.

Mr Butler scratched his neck. "Nails, glass, and pieces of wire often find their way into tyres."

Sam raised his eyebrows. "But not ones which have been inflated and put directly into the back of a vehicle."

"Point taken." Mr Butler made a note on the clipboard he carried. "Anything else?"

Sam lifted a jerry can out of the back. "This was empty. I believe someone poured the diesel away."

"Or forgot to fill it up in the first place," Mr Butler countered. Thabiti felt his cheeks burn and he turned away from the car. This was a waste of time, as he would still be blamed whatever evidence Sam provided.

"Have you spoken to Mr Obado?" Sam drew himself to his full height and widened his stance.

Mr Butler's jaw tightened. "I haven't had a chance yet."

"But you are one of his customers?"

"Yes." Mr Butler leaned back.

"And have you ever found his work slovenly or for him to forget simple procedures?"

"Well, no."

Sam brought his feet together. "I called Mr Obado, who is appalled at what happened. And he personally checked the vehicle and all the parts, including the spare tyre and fuel cans. He said the winch strop was brand new and arrived two weeks ago from the UK, via Kesom freight. When I examined the winch strop, the stitching had given way, but not all the threads were frayed. I believe some of them had been cut."

"Are you accusing someone of deliberately tampering with the strop?" Mr Butler sucked in his cheeks.

"Well it's either that or Mr Obado received a faulty one from the UK. Besides, he confirmed Thabiti's testimony that they tested the strop and winch cable last week."

"That's a serious allegation."

"With serious consequences."

The two men eyed each other.

Thabiti felt his legs shake and his mouth was dry. His voice cracked as he asked, "What about the electrical connectors?"

"What about them?" asked Mr Butler sharply.

"Someone deliberately unhooked them before the scrutineering." Thabiti showed Mr Butler the photo he'd taken.

Mr Butler looked at Thabiti and back to Sam. "Neither of you did this?" They stared back at him.

"And someone hid our team's safety equipment," added Thabiti.

"OK, I agree, it does look like someone tried to stop your team taking part. But the winch strop is a serious matter. Do you have any idea who might have done this?"

Thabiti looked at Sam and away again as Sam said, "We're not sure, but at the moment, I would like you to clear Thabiti of neglecting his duties and causing the accident which injured, and potentially, killed Mayur Chauhan."

Mr Butler hesitated. "I've known Mr Obado a long time, and you're right, he would not send a car to the Rhino Charge without meticulous preparation and checks. Was the car transported here directly from Nanyuki on a truck?"

"Yes," confirmed Thabiti as he twirled his phone in his hand. "And it was unloaded at the Bandit Bush Hog's camp where it stayed until scrutineering, and after that it was parked in here."

"Ok, this is what I can do for you." Mr Butler held his clipboard to his chest. "I'll write an official report stating the facts you've given me. And I will express my opinion that the incidents were not due to any neglect or omission of the mechanic's duties, but as a direct result of sabotage by a person, or persons unknown."

Thabiti sank to his knees and held his head in his hands. He felt drained, but he had been cleared. The accident was not his fault.

CHAPTER THIRTY-FOUR

Rose was reluctant to leave the peace of the escarpment and return to the bustling headquarters. At the Rhino Charge camp, the cricket match had finished and most of the participants had left. Three children still ran around playing tag.

"Wait here," requested Marina. "I'll fetch cousin Aatma."

Marina returned and beckoned to Rose. "Come in. Aatma is here with my older cousin, Hinesh, but the rest of the family, including Uncle Deepak, are away visiting friends in another camp."

They found Aatma reading a book, and Hinesh bent over some paperwork, at the table in the central marquee. Marina had told Rose that Aatma was forty, but up close he looked older. His shaved head did little to conceal his thinning hair and his eyes were red-rimmed and surrounded by sallow yellow skin.

Aatma looked up and grinned at Marina. "You're in trouble. Your father was furious when he found out you'd disappeared. He was all for finding that young man of yours and giving him a beating."

Marina bristled and replied, "I'm not fifteen and Thabiti has enough problems at the moment."

Turning to Rose, Aatma asked, "Do you mind if I smoke? I try not to when the family are around as they disapprove." He cradled a mug of black coffee in his left hand.

Rose sat down and asked, "Were you out celebrating last night?"

"Something like that." Aatma dragged on his cigarette. "Thabiti's your team's mechanic, isn't he? Is he being blamed for causing yesterday's accident?"

Marina's face reddened and she retorted, "You mean is he being blamed for Mayur's death? He did nothing wrong. It's just that he's an easy target."

Aatma shrugged his shoulders. "I'm sure it will soon blow over. We all know the risks involved when we sign up for the Rhino Charge."

Rose was irritated by Aatma's indifference. "Risks are one thing, deliberately interfering with a car and its equipment is quite another."

Aatma blew out smoke and eyed Rose. "Are you telling me someone tampered with the winch? Who would do that?"

Rose's eyes narrowed as she stared at Aatma. "We wondered if you might be able to tell us."

Aatma shoved his chair back and knocked over his coffee cup. Black liquid sloshed onto the table. "Hey, lady. Don't start pointing the finger at me. I haven't been near the Bandit Bush Hogs or their car."

"Then you can confirm you didn't damage their car or the winch equipment."

Flustered, Aatma leapt to his feet. "I had nothing to do with this."

"Aatma, calm down." Marina's voice was soothing. She'd found a cloth and was mopping up the spilt coffee.

He turned on her and sneered, "It's easy for you to say. None of this affects you."

Marina bristled and threw down the cloth. "It does, actually. Whilst Thabiti is accused of neglecting his duties and causing the crash, Baba has banned me from seeing him."

Cousin Aatma paced up and down in front of the mess tent and lit another cigarette. "Sorry Marina, I didn't mean to snap at you. I get rather uptight about car accidents."

Rose looked across at Aatma and asked, "Is that because of the one you were involved in twenty years ago?"

Aatma stopped. "How do you know about that? What has Jono Urquhart been saying?"

Marina answered him. "Jono hardly says anything at the moment, he's so miserable. I told Mama Rose about cousin Vadhana and the crash."

Aatma's hand shook violently. "You shouldn't have."

"Why?" Marina flopped into a chair. "Mama Rose thinks what happened yesterday is connected to your crash."

"My crash? Why do you call it that? How can the two be connected?"

Rose leaned back, laced her hands together and declared, "Because I believe Jono Urquhart's return is the trigger which resulted in Mayur's death."

They all jumped as Hinesh slapped his hands on the table. "It's a good job Mayur Chauhan is dead or I would kill him myself. Can you believe it, he's been muscling in on the Belmont Hotel group's account and he's seriously undercutting us. The manager at the Suffolk sent me these figures, Aatma."

Hinesh waved the papers in the air. "There's no way he's making a profit at these prices. And I bet Kumar knows nothing about it. He thinks he still runs the business, but Mayur did plenty behind his back. I for one won't be grieving over his death."

Aatma slumped into a chair, removed his glasses and rubbed his eyes. Marina put her arm around him. "I know it's hard, but please can you tell Mama Rose about the crash?"

"OK, as long as you fetch me a Tusker."

Aatma began, "It was twenty years ago. Vadhana and I were in the UK and we visited Jono at his college. It was one of those cold but bright winter days, when the entire landscape is tinged with white. Unfortunately, it extended onto the road, and the car hit a patch of ice, skidded out of control, and we hit a tree."

Aatma took a long swig from the open bottle Marina handed him. "I couldn't get to Vadhana in the passenger seat, but I was worried about Jono who was unconscious and had a large gash on his head. I panicked and pulled him from the car, but I couldn't wake him. When the police arrived, they asked me some questions before Jono and I were taken to hospital in an ambulance. That was the last I saw of Vadhana."

He took another slurp. "I wasn't badly injured, but they kept me in for observation. Poor Jono had a swelling on his brain, so they had to operate on him to relieve it. I visited him before I was discharged, but he was still unconscious. And then I returned home with Vadhana's body and didn't see him again. He was tried, convicted, and given a two-year suspended sentence. I was told he remained in the UK, working on a farm in Scotland, and the next time I heard about him, he was a pilot in New Zealand. It was a shock when Da told me he was back in Kenya, flying planes for Equator Air."

"Do you still blame him for the accident? And for your sister's death?"

Aatma reached for his cigarettes. "It happened so long ago. Why can't you leave it alone?"

CHAPTER THIRTY-FIVE

Marina and Rose left Aatma to his beer and cigarettes and went in search of Sam and Thabiti.

"Rose," Nick West called as they passed the registration tent. "Kumar Chauhan persuaded the Nairobi medical officer to fly down and examine Mayur's body in situ, before returning with it to Nairobi. I wondered if you could look after him, as we have a problem with a couple of the GPS units, which I need to unravel for the scorers."

She had plenty to do helping clear Thabiti's name, but accompanying the medical officer might offer some insights into Mayur's death, so she asked, "When is he due to arrive?"

"Within the next half hour. Why don't you wait in the catering area, and I'll send someone to find you when he arrives."

Marina touched Rose's arm, and said, "I've spotted Sam and Thabiti. Shall we join them?"

Thabiti appeared to be making up for the meals he'd missed the day before as he tucked into a steak sandwich.

Rose stole a chip as she sat down. She explained, "I've been asked to wait here for the Nairobi medical officer and accompany him when he examines Mayur's body."

Thabiti had been about to bite into his sandwich, but put it down. "Do you mind? I'm eating." He lifted the sandwich to his mouth and as he bit into it, pieces of coleslaw dropped out.

"We have some good news." Sam looked at Thabiti and shook his head. "But you've probably guessed that."

Marina leant forward and asked eagerly, "Have you found out who interfered with the car?"

Sam rested his arms on the table. "I'm afraid not, but at least Thabiti has been cleared. Well, that is to say the official report, which Frank Butler is writing, will state that the winch strop was deliberately tampered with. And he agreed to write that in his opinion the accident had nothing to do with Thabiti neglecting his duties. As you can see, Thabiti is very relieved."

They all laughed, but then Rose remembered Mayur. "We still need to find out who sabotaged the car, as it did lead to Mayur's death."

Thabiti spluttered, "But why does that matter now? I'm no longer being blamed for it."

Rose turned to him. "I know you're not being implicated in Frank's report, but that could change if the police are involved. You see, they don't know you, or Sam or Mr Obado, and they may not understand the nuances of the accident. Think about it. They will be faced with a team which appears to have neglected its vehicle or a phantom saboteur. Which route will they choose?"

The colour drained from Thabiti's face. "I think I'm going to be sick."

"No you're not," chided Rose, and she ate another chip.

The group was silent.

Sam spoke. "Thabiti and I don't have the answer. We still don't know who caused the damage. But did you find anything out?"

Rose caught Marina's eye and said, "We should tell them. I'm not sure how, but I still think it is behind this weekend's events."

Marina took a deep breath and told Sam and Thabiti about their conversation with her cousin Aatma and the car accident. Rose munched on Thabiti's chips.

When Marina finished, Thabiti said, "I still don't see how, or when, anyone from the Rhino Force team gained access to the car or its equipment."

The group was silent again.

Sam sat back, crossed his arms, and asked, "Thabiti, are you suggesting it was an inside job? That one of your own teammates vandalised their own vehicle? But that doesn't make sense."

"It wasn't me!' cried Marina.

Rose placed a hand on her arm. "Nobody is accusing you, and anyway, you and Sam joined the team at the last minute."

"And it wasn't Thabiti," added Marina, looking across at him.

Sam pondered the problem aloud. "Why would Kumar or Mayur sabotage their own car? All they needed to do was fail to fulfil their financial pledge and they wouldn't be able to start."

"Lucky I found that cheque." Thabiti's appetite had returned and he dipped a chip into tomato ketchup. He looked up as everyone stared at him.

"What cheque?" asked Rose.

Thabiti twirled his chip. "The one Jono collected in Nanyuki before flying you and Chloe down here. He'd lost it, but I found it in the tube with the sponsor's banner," Thabiti told his rapt audience.

Rose tapped the table. "Jono's a different person from the one who flew us down."

Sam added, "And he's likely to know about engines, being a bush pilot. He also had the opportunity."

"But what would Jono have to gain?" Marina asked.

Rose looked up at the sky and responded, "It's not necessarily what he, or anyone else, had to gain, but what they had to lose. And that comes back to your family's secret." She looked across at Marina.

"Rose," a loud, bossy voice called.

"That's Tanya West. I guess it's time to meet the medical officer," explained Rose.

"You can't leave now," cried Thabiti. "We need to get to the bottom of this."

"Then put your thinking caps on. Nobody's leaving headquarters… apart from poor Mayur."

CHAPTER THIRTY-SIX

The Nairobi medical officer was a white-haired African man with a lined face and a brisk manner. He shook Rose's proffered hand and said, "Let's get on with it. Where's the body?"

Rose led him to the medical tent. Although the zip on the tent flap was pulled closed, Rose could hear the drone of flies inside.

She opened the flap and stood back so the medical officer could enter.

He said, "Keeping corpses in hot weather is not a good idea, but when there is no choice… " He shooed the flies away and lifted the sheet. Rose moved towards him, but he raised a hand. "Please wait for me outside."

Rose was annoyed at being dismissed. She wanted to know what was happening, and kept glancing inside, but all she saw was the medical officer leaning over the mound of Mayur's body. She spotted an empty chair under the shade of a tree and sat down.

The medical officer poked his head out of the tent. "Who was in the other bed and when did they leave?"

"It was an injured teammate and I'm not sure when he

left, but probably somewhere between nine and ten last night." The medical officer ducked back into the tent.

Rose kicked at some cigarette butts and wondered what Craig was doing. She checked her watch and saw it was midday. He was probably working on a crossword puzzle and looking forward to his lunch. She needed to organise some trips so he could catch up with friends, and it would be lovely to return to some of his most loved areas of Kenya.

Next month was the Lewa Marathon, which was another event they had both officiated at for years. In the past they had camped overnight with friends so they were ready for the marathon's seven o'clock start. They manned a water station and handed out drinks and energy snacks to the competitors.

But Craig could not camp now, and the lodges would be full over the marathon weekend. She wondered if she could negotiate a deal for them both to stay a few nights in Lewa after the marathon.

The medical officer called to her. "I'm nearly finished. Can you find the car which brought me, and some askaris to carry the body."

Rose stood and straightened her light green shirt. She found the car and the driver leaning against it chatting to his friends. She rounded them all up and returned to the medical tent. The men accompanied the medical examiner and came back carrying a black body bag.

"I'm heading straight to the airstrip so as not to lose any more time," the medical officer informed her as he climbed into the car.

"So what should I tell the organisers, and Kumar Chauhan?"

"Tell them the cause of death is inconclusive, but I will know soon after I start my examination in Nairobi. I will contact them later," he shouted as the car drove away.

CHAPTER THIRTY-SEVEN

R ose returned to the catering area and found Chloe with
Thabiti and Sam. Chloe had showered and looked a
different person from earlier in the morning, with sleek hair
and designer shorts and top. She greeted Rose with a grin.
"What was the verdict? A vampire struck at midnight or he
was stung by a gigantuous mosquito?"

"Don't be silly," quipped Rose. "And where's Marina?"

Thabiti didn't look up from his phone, but responded,
"She went back to her camp for lunch. She's going to see if
she can find out any more about the car tampering."

Sam frowned. "I hope she treads carefully like a cheetah
stalking its prey, or she may become the target."

Thabiti put his phone on the table and asked, "What did
the medical officer say?"

"That the cause of death was inconclusive and he would
provide a clearer answer later today, after examining the body
in Nairobi," replied Rose.

"Which gives us time to solve the mystery of the
sabotaged car." Chloe's voice was bright, but Thabiti and
Sam both rested their chins in their upturned palms and
looked dejected.

Rose looked at them both and said, "So I take it you're no further forward discovering who's our man?"

They shook their heads.

Sam sat up. "What did you mean when you said it might not be what someone has to gain but what they have to lose? And why do you think sabotaging our team's car is linked to the earlier accident which killed Marina's cousin?"

Rose looked at Chloe. "It's OK. They've already told me all about it."

Rose considered the question and replied, "Jono's return disturbed a long-buried secret. And I believe it triggered these events. Jono's here, at a car rally, with his old school friends, and the family of the girl he killed."

Sam sat back and crossed his arms. "Jono lost his whole life because of that crash. What else has he left to lose?"

Rose raised her hands. "Everything! He's been away from Kenya for twenty years. The accident happened in the UK. Deepak was in mourning for his daughter and is unlikely to have broadcast details of the crash. And Jono was put on trial in the UK and given a suspended sentence."

"Which does not have to be declared after the period of the sentence has passed," Sam commented.

Rose looked at him. "I didn't know that. So probably only Deepak Seth's family knew he was convicted of a crime of killing someone in a car accident."

"Blackmail," declared Chloe.

"What?" asked Thabiti, picking up his phone.

"Someone blackmailed Jono to tamper with the car and threatened to expose his past if he didn't agree. If details of his conviction leaked out, he'd probably lose his job and be forced to leave Kenya again." She clasped her hands together. "The poor man's been too afraid to return home for twenty years and when he does, the car accident is here to haunt him."

Thabiti was deep in thought as he fiddled with his phone. "He helped me check the car and I left the bonnet raised when I stopped for lunch on Friday. He could easily have disconnected the electrical connectors then. But when did he tamper with the winch strop as the container was usually locked?"

"Of course," exclaimed Rose. "He had it wrapped around his waist on Monday morning when you walked past us. I saw the yellow end dangling under his team shirt."

Thabiti bit his lip. "He could have removed it on Sunday after completing the scrutineering checks and returned it on Monday morning."

Sam grunted. "He will have used that penknife he carries to cut the stitching."

Chloe wrinkled her nose. "But it was an enormous risk. I'm sure he didn't want to harm anyone."

Rose turned to her and explained, "He would be running out of options. Thabiti found the cheque he'd deliberately mislaid, and he and Sam found and reconnected the electrical cables. I don't think winching is usually done on such a steep slope. So normally if a winch broke, a car would crash onto some rocks or into a tree, which might stop it continuing, but would be unlikely to hurt anyone. No wonder Jono was pacing up and down on Monday when Mayur was driving the car down the slope."

Chloe touched Rose's arm. "So it's not surprising he was in shock afterwards." She looked at Sam and Thabiti. "But if we all agree he had nothing to gain by tampering with the car and was acting under duress, who was blackmailing him?"

Rose slapped her thighs. "All roads lead back to the Seths: Uncle Deepak, the bitter father of the victim; Marina's oldest cousin, Hinesh, who also blames Jono for killing his sister and for the near collapse of the family business; and quiet bespectacled Aatma, Jono's old friend, who blames him for killing his sister.

"How do you intend to approach the Seths?" asked Chloe.

"Head on with my own rhino. Are you up for it, Sam?"

Sam broke into a broad smile.

CHAPTER THIRTY-EIGHT

Rose turned to Sam as they strode towards the Rhino Force camp. "Of course, we don't have any actual powers to investigate or question the Seth family."

"Actually, that's not entirely true. I may be a member of Kenya's Anti-Poaching Unit, but I'm also an officer in the Kenya Wildlife Service. We have certain delegated powers, although they are really for wildlife-related crimes, but I can be persuasive."

Rose realised she knew very little about Sam and each time they met, which usually involved a murder investigation, she peeled away another layer and learnt something new about him. "I had no idea you were an officer in the KWS, but I suppose I should have guessed."

Sam smiled. "Craig did. He asked me directly at the Laikipia Conservation Society conference last month."

Entering the Rhino Charge camp, through the gazebo, they found the Seths seated around a long dining table in the central marquee. As Sam and Rose approached, the children pushed back their chairs and ran to a tent. Marina's head was bowed, but she peered across at Rose.

"What do you want?" Deepak called. "You're disturbing our lunch."

Sam took the lead. "This is official business. We'll be happy to wait until you've finished your meal."

Deepak raised his hands. "Ah, there's no point delaying whatever you have to say. Sit down." All the women, except Marina, rose from the table. Her mother tugged her sleeve, but Marina refused to move.

Rose began. "The Nairobi medical officer collected Mayur Chauhan's body earlier and he's promised to provide the results of the autopsy later today."

"That will be a relief to Kumar, but it's no concern of mine." Deepak spooned his remaining curry into his mouth.

"It is," Sam looked around the table, "if you, or one of your team members, coerced another person to interfere with the Bandit Bush Hog's team car, and its equipment, causing yesterday's accident, and the death of Mayur Chauhan."

Aatma lit a cigarette.

"Not at the table," Deepak remonstrated.

Aatma stood and began pacing in front of the tent.

Marina's older cousin Hinesh removed a Tusker from the cool box. He challenged, "What are you talking about? That useless boyfriend of my cousin's was responsible for the accident." He glared at Marina.

Sam said in a voice of authority, "A senior Rhino Charge official examined the car and evidence of earlier interference. He agreed that the winch strop had been deliberately interfered with and it caused yesterday's accident."

Hinesh banged a fist on the table. "Are you accusing one of us of damaging their car?"

Rose remained calm. "Perhaps, but as you had limited access, we believe one of you paid or threatened someone else to do it for you."

"Get out," shouted Deepak. He was red in the face. "You

have no authority to come into our camp throwing around such allegations."

Beside her Sam growled.

Hinesh leant towards her. "Why would any of us bother? We have a great car. A great team. And we are in the running to win this year's competition."

"Congratulations," said Rose flatly. "But it will be only the second time you've beaten Kumar's Bandit Bush Hog team since you started competing. So I think one of you wanted to stack the odds in your favour."

At the end of the table, Deepak flexed his fingers in anger.

"Who caused the damage?" Hinesh asked.

"We believe it was Jono Urquhart."

Deepak flinched and Aatma strode into the middle of the camp. Hinesh hissed, "Don't mention that man's name to this family."

"Because of the accident?"

"Yes, and if you know about that, you'll know why he's the last person any of this family associate with."

"Except if they wanted to get their own back by blackmailing him." Rose's words hung in the air.

Hinesh shifted uncomfortably in his chair.

Deepak appeared unmoved. He sat taller with his shoulders back and his chest and chin thrust forward.

Rose asked him, "When did you find out Jono was back in Kenya?"

"Why do you need to know? It's enough that he's here, larger than life, flying around in aeroplanes." Deepak spat on the floor.

"That must have annoyed you."

"It did. I wasn't too bothered when he fled to Scotland or was hiding in New Zealand, but now he's back and still denying any knowledge of the accident which killed my darling daughter."

Rose felt a knot in her belly. "So you have met him? Spoken to him?"

Deepak crossed his arms. "I bumped into him at the Aero Club at Wilson Airport."

Hinesh looked at their father. "You didn't tell us that."

Deepak said defiantly, "I don't have to tell you everything."

Aatma walked towards his father. "Did you suggest he try and get a place on Kumar's team?"

Deepak raised his hands and stuck out his bottom lip. "I might have mentioned in passing that Kumar needed a navigator."

Marina had been impassive during the exchange, but now her eyes narrowed. "I was delighted when Thabiti was invited to join the Bandit Bush Hogs, but surprised as he had no experience as a mechanic. Was that your doing, Uncle Deepak?"

Deepak sneered. "All it took was a phone call to their usual mechanic's employer. I asked them to play around with the work schedule so he would be out of the country during the Charge. I told Jono to find a keen but inexperienced young man to be their team's mechanic."

Marina turned to her father who was glancing around in confusion. "You see, Baba, you thought Thabiti was useless and not fit for this family. Well, you're right about the last part. He's too good for us." Marina threw back her chair and ran out of the camp.

Her father watched her leave, open-mouthed.

CHAPTER THIRTY-NINE

Hinesh walked towards his father, leant against a chair, and asked, "Da, are the allegations true? Did you persuade Jono Urquhart to sabotage Kumar Chauhan's team car?"

Deepak's lip curled into a smirk. "So what if I did? Have you seen the way Kumar laughs at me every time we meet?"

Hinesh straightened up. "That's because you refuse to be civil and it's become a sport to him. I do understand, but Nairobi is a small place and we all have to get along. Anyway, you always grunt or snarl at him."

Hinesh ran his hand through his hair. "I'm no fan of the Chauhans, and Kumar made life very difficult for us when he set up his business, but that is not the same as deliberately interfering with a vehicle in the Rhino Charge. This event is dangerous enough without tampering with equipment. Do you realise your action has led to Mayur's death?"

"Then Kumar will know what it's like to lose a child," Deepak spat.

Sam asked, "Mr Seth, did you mean to injure Mayur Chauhan or any other member of the Bandit Bush Hog team?"

"No, of course not." Deepak gripped his hands together. "If that over-zealous mechanic hadn't found the cheque, the team wouldn't have started. I didn't mean for anyone to die."

Deepak slumped into his chair, his bravado spent. "Living with death eats away at you. It's a living hell."

Hinesh moved and sat beside his father. "What did you say to Jono?"

"I told him that unless he made sure Kumar's team didn't beat us this year I would let it be known he was a convicted murderer."

Sam stood. "Can I confirm the facts, Mr Seth? You blackmailed Jono Urquhart, and you threatened to expose his criminal conviction in the UK, unless he helped the Rhino Force team beat the Bandit Bush Hogs."

Deepak interrupted. "He was only supposed to ensure they didn't take part, or if they did, that they didn't complete the course."

Sam continued, "So after his initial attempts failed, he damaged vital equipment which caused a horrendous crash."

"That's on his own head. I never meant it to happen." Deepak looked down at the floor.

Sam widened his stance. "Did you forbid him from damaging equipment?"

Deepak shook his head and mumbled, "No, but I didn't mean him to go that far."

Rose interjected. "You threatened to ruin his life for a second time?" She was angry. "How far did you think he would go?" There was silence.

"I can't believe this," exclaimed Hinesh. "Now I'll have to go to the organisers and withdraw from the Rhino Charge."

"Why?" Deepak looked up and rubbed his forehead.

"Because any prize would be too bitter to accept." It was Hinesh's turn to shake his head. "And this year I finally thought we had a chance of winning. We had a great run."

CHAPTER FORTY

R ose felt despondent as she and Sam left the Rhino Force camp. A tragedy had driven Deepak Seth to become a bitter old man. And he'd preyed on Jono Urquhart's guilt and remorse, to coerce him into helping Rhino Force in a car rally by interfering with a vehicle, which led to the death of someone else's child, in another car accident. There was so much heartache and misery.

She stood to one side, allowing Hinesh past as he hurried in the direction of the registration tent.

Sam looked back, waited for her, and commented, "You're very quiet and withdrawn. Are you saddened by Deepak Seth's actions?"

She smiled weakly at him. "Don't worry. It's just the musings of an old woman. You see, I can accept death in its many forms, but it's the damaging effect on the living I struggle to understand. When our lives pass so quickly, why spend them in bitterness and mourning, or consumed by guilt? It seems such a waste."

As they reached the centre of the headquarters, Nick West spotted her, raised his hand, and came to meet them. "Rose, may I have a quiet word?" He looked at Sam. "In private."

She stood a little taller and looked Nick in the eye. "Sam is a KWS officer and I trust him implicitly. Whatever you have to tell me, you can say in his presence."

Nick ran his tongue over his lips. "It's about the Nairobi medical officer. By the way, thank you for looking after him. He must be back in Nairobi now, as he's emailed me his initial findings about Mayur Chauhan's death."

"That was quick."

Nick shuffled his feet. "The thing is, Mayur Chauhan didn't die of internal bleeding, or in fact from any of his wounds from the car crash. He was suffocated."

"That's unexpected." It was all Rose could think to say. She considered the medical officer's visit and realised he'd probably deduced the cause of death at the scene, but needed to check for internal damage and bleeding back in Nairobi.

"I'm not sure what to do next." Nick looked from Rose to Sam and back again. "Should I contact the police in Narok? Or is this a matter for the Criminal Investigation Department? What do you think?"

"I have no idea," replied Rose. She looked at Sam.

He chewed his finger and then said, "I doubt either organisation will travel today, as it'll be dark by the time they arrive. The problem we have is that tomorrow the competitors pack up and leave. And I can't see how we or the police can stop them." Sam shrugged his shoulders.

Nick rubbed his forehead. "We've postponed the prize-giving until tomorrow morning. I thought it the right thing to do under the circumstances, a mark of respect. Besides, a lot of noise and celebration tonight by the winning teams would be inappropriate."

Rose responded, "That's a kind gesture, which I'm sure Lavanya and Kumar Chauhan will appreciate."

Nick glanced around uneasily. "Rose, in light of the medical officer's findings, I have two favours to ask of you."

He held her gaze. "Firstly, can I ask you to break the news about the cause of death to Kumar and Mayur's wife? I froze earlier and you did a really great job. You were calm and sympathetic."

Rose nodded. "Of course. I'll do that straight away. What was the second thing?"

"Frank told me you've recently helped the police with a couple of murder investigations in Nanyuki: Aisha Onyango's death and the murder of Davina Dijan at the Giant's Club Summit. So is there any chance you could look into this case? I fear your friend is right."

Nick looked apologetically at Sam. "The police will arrive too late to solve the case, or they will act in haste and focus on an easy target, and arrest the wrong person."

Sam spoke in an authoritative tone. "I will be happy to assist Mama Rose. And I have contacts with both the Narok police and CID."

Nick grasped Rose's hand, squeezing lightly, and did the same with Sam's. "Thanks so much. It's a great weight off my shoulders, although I suspect I shall have to deal with whatever you do or don't find out tomorrow. But at least I can complete my Rhino Charge business."

CHAPTER FORTY-ONE

R ose and Sam returned once again, through the leleshwa bushes, to the Bandit Bush Hog's camp, where the atmosphere was sombre. The tents had been re-erected under the desert date trees and the bags stowed away.

The staff and cooking area behind the thorny bushes was silent. The only people who seemed to be around were Kumar and Jono, who sat quietly at either end of the table in the events shelter. Jono nursed a Tusker whilst Kumar leaned back in his chair, staring into space.

Rose coughed, but Kumar did not move. "What is it? Can an old man not mourn his son in peace?"

"Pole, bwana." Rose's words were soft.

Kumar turned his head to focus on her. "Mama Rose, please accept my apologies, but I was not expecting you." He pressed his lips together when he spotted Sam.

"I'm afraid we are the bearers of more sad tidings. Is Lavanya here?"

Lavanya appeared at the entrance of a nearby tent. "Come here, my dear," requested Kumar.

They all sat down at the table although Jono remained detached and continued to stare at his beer bottle.

Rose turned to Kumar and began, "Nick West wanted me to pass on his thanks for organising the Nairobi medical officer. The officer was unable to tell us anything when he was here, but he returned with Mayur's body to Nairobi. And he's just sent Nick the results of his examination. Has he also spoken to you?

"Neither Nick nor the medical officer have contacted me." Kumar tapped the table. "So they sent you in their place?"

"Something like that." Rose floundered but there was no easy way to say this. "Mayur did not die as a result of his injuries from the car crash. He was suffocated."

At the far end of the table, Jono knocked his Tusker bottle to the floor. Lavanya gasped and the colour drained from her face. Kumar's body was rigid whilst his eyes swivelled from Rose to Sam and back again. He did not, or could not, speak.

Rose placed a hand on Kumar's arm. "I'm sorry I couldn't find an easier way to break the news. We've all been focusing on the accident and how it was caused, so this news came as a shock."

Kumar ran his tongue along his lips. "I don't understand. How was he suffocated?" Lavanya and Jono both stared down at the table.

"If you don't have any objections, Nick West has asked Sam and I to try and find that out."

"But Mama Rose, you are not a policeman. How can you?"

Sam answered. "Mr Chauhan, I'm afraid the police may arrive too late to complete a proper investigation, as all the competitors leave tomorrow. I am a KWS officer, and did you know Mama Rose recently solved two murders in Nanyuki?"

Rose fidgeted with her hands, feeling the colour rise in her cheeks.

Kumar leaned back, his eyes wide. "Two?"

Rose was unsure if he was surprised by her sleuthing abilities or the number of murders in her home town.

Kumar looked around the camp. "Of course you are right. Tomorrow morning this will all be dismantled and everyone will leave, giving the police precious little to investigate. But my oldest son has been killed, murdered. I need to know who committed this terrible act and why."

Kumar stared at Sam and grunted. "You have depths I had not perceived. I give you my blessing to find my son's killer as long as you promise to keep Mama Rose safe. I do not need her on my conscience as well."

CHAPTER FORTY-TWO

Thabiti didn't feel like returning to his camp, and neither did Marina. They found a table in the catering area away from the bar and those competitors and supporters who were finishing a late lunch. Thabiti picked at a chocolate muffin whilst Marina sipped a passion fruit juice.

Marina moaned, "My family's such a mess."

"No family's perfect," he commiserated. "Look at mine. My father did a runner, my mother was murdered, and my sister's crazy."

"Pearl's not crazy. The events surrounding your mother's death were distressing, and she just needs time to recover. Is she home alone?" Marina circled her straw through her deep orange-coloured juice.

"No, Dr Farrukh persuaded her to return to the Cottage Hospital for a few days. I'm afraid my working at Mr Obado's garage all day didn't help Pearl, and her recovery faltered. Besides, I was able to give Doris a much-needed week off." He found a chocolate chip and extracted it from his muffin.

"Is she eating properly?"

"Pearl? Well not what I would call eating, but I suppose

it's a start. She skips breakfast and asks Doris to prepare her a salad for lunch. Doris insists on a hot meal at night with plenty of meat, which suits me. What's not so good are the cakes Doris has started baking to tempt her. I end up finishing them, which isn't good for my waistline." He looked down at his tummy.

Marina playfully patted it and said, "I thought you'd started cycling?"

"I ride my bike to Mr Obado's garage, but I haven't been on any longer rides. I want to explore some of the tracks on Mount Kenya after I've recovered from the Rhino Charge. That is, as long as I'm free to do so." Thabiti rested his hand on his chin. Would he ever be free of suspicion for causing Mayur's car accident?

Marina rubbed his back. "Don't worry. You haven't done anything wrong."

"But the police might not see it that way."

"I'm sure they will, but then what?" Marina sipped her juice. "I feel so lost at the moment. You, me, and Pearl. We're all in our early twenties and we should be grabbing hold of life, gaining new experiences and trying to make a difference in the world. I shouldn't be sitting around waiting for my father to introduce me to some fat boring man he wants me to marry."

Thabiti sat up. "No way!"

Marina had a pained expression as she slumped back in her chair. "He's arranged someone for me to meet when we get home and he's told me to give up my safari and lodge work."

"So will you?" Thabiti bit his lip. Marina loved her work and he was certain she didn't want to stop it.

Marina twirled her straw. "I'm not sure."

Their conversation was interrupted by a short, stocky man who pulled up a chair and addressed Marina.

"There you are. I've been trying to call you."

Marina patted her pockets. "I must have left my phone back at our camp. Sorry, I left in a bit of a hurry."

"Is everything all right?" the man asked.

She looked at him forlornly. "Not really. Our team car had a nasty accident in the Charge yesterday. Only the driver was inside and we thought his injuries weren't too bad. That is until we found out he'd died during the night. It's rather a mess."

She raised a hand toward Thabiti. "Sorry, this is Thabiti, one of my teammates." She turned to Thabiti and moved her hand across towards the new arrival. "This is Ollie. He works for Kifaru Safaris, who have lodges across Kenya and Tanzania. He sometimes gives me work."

Thabiti returned to the dissection of his muffin, and tried to ignore Ollie.

He heard him say. "But that's terrible. How did it happen?"

While Marina explained the previous day's accident, Thabiti thought about Pearl. She couldn't keep returning to the Cottage Hospital every time he went away. Besides, Marina was right, it was now time for him to decide what he wanted to do, whether he should return to university or look for a job. But he didn't want to leave Pearl all alone. He didn't mind being by himself, and in Nairobi he'd usually avoided social situations.

He found it better in Nanyuki, probably because the town was smaller, and the people friendlier and more helpful. But he didn't think social isolation was good for Pearl, so how should he introduce her back into the community? Previously, she'd shunned the less glamorous people of Nanyuki, but surely it would be a bad idea for her to return to the glitzy parties in Nairobi?

"So you see," he heard Ollie say, "we need a relief

manager while we invite and vet applicants for a permanent position."

"The lodge is in Borana?" asked Marina. "I don't know that area."

"Borana is in Laikipia, adjacent to the Lewa Conservancy, and together they form a UNESCO Heritage Site. A few years ago the two conservancies removed their boundary fences and became the largest rhino sanctuary in Kenya. They have over a hundred black and eighty white rhino."

Thabiti watched the gleam return to Marina's eyes as she sat up. "It sounds fascinating. And this is a brand new lodge?"

Ollie replied, "The family who own it, who would prefer to remain anonymous, bought a twenty-year lease from the Borana Conservancy. They built the main house for themselves for when they visit Kenya, and there are various self-contained cottages. It's very upmarket and exclusive, and the family expect high quality food and service. We've already employed a top class chef from the Suffolk Hotel in Nairobi."

Marina smoothed her t-shirt. "It sounds rather intimidating."

Ollie leaned towards her. "You'll be fine. There'll only be the family staying at the beginning, as well as a small yoga retreat in the studio. There is one other thing. They have a high end solar and generator set up which is rather complex, so they do need someone who knows a bit about electrics and mechanics. The installer is willing to teach you how to use and repair the system."

Marina's eyes bulged. "I'm no good at that sort of thing. It's more Thabiti's area of expertise. He's our team mechanic."

Thabiti looked up to find Ollie assessing him. Ollie turned back to Marina. "That's excellent. The family would prefer a couple." Ollie blushed. "Not that you have to be romantically attached or anything, but there are some roles they would prefer a man to oversee and for others they prefer a woman's touch. They can be a bit demanding, but the pay is excellent."

Marina turned to Thabiti. "What do you think?"

He looked at Marina with a feeling of being trapped. What was she volunteering him for? "What exactly are your proposing?"

Marina was beaming. "That you and I spend a month looking after an upmarket lodge on Borana Conservancy. The money is great, enough to support me for the rest of the year. So then I'll be able to stand up to my father, and tell him I'm not giving up my job or marrying some man he's chosen for me. Please, Thabiti. This means a lot to me."

Thabiti looked around. He could leave now, but Marina would never speak to him again. This job was clearly important to her. He muttered, "I'm not very good with strangers. I don't mind sorting out electrical issues or dealing with security, but I don't want to serve drinks or be gracious to people."

"Don't worry," chuckled Ollie. "The family won't expect you to eat with them or anything like that."

Thabiti remembered Pearl. "But I can't leave Pearl at home or at the Cottage Hospital for a month."

"Who's Pearl?" asked Ollie.

"My sister. She recently suffered a personal tragedy."

"Well, I'm sure she can join you. There's lots of space and it might be good for her."

"Fantastic." Marina clapped her hands. "Talking of safaris, I really need to get out of here. How long are you around for?"

Ollie checked his watch. "Oops, I should have been at a meeting five minutes ago. And then I'm catching up with friends for supper, so I'm here a while."

"Do you mind if I borrow your car and take Thabiti and some friends out for a game drive and sundowners?"

"Sure." He tossed her a set of keys on a beaded key ring. "I've parked near the entrance. It's one of the safari Land Cruisers, with the company logo on the side."

CHAPTER FORTY-THREE

Rose and Sam weaved through the mostly empty tables towards Thabiti and Marina. Staff from the Rusty Nail Caterers wandered around with dustbin bags, collecting empty paper plates and scrunched-up napkins. They tipped the contents of used paper and plastic cups onto the sandy ground before adding them to their black sacks.

Rose watched a stocky man leave as they approached. She asked, "Who was that?"

Marina grabbed Rose's arm. "My... sorry, our, new temporary boss. Thabiti and I've been offered a month's work looking after a luxury family home and lodge in Borana."

Thabiti's lips were pressed together in a slight grimace.

Sam looked across at him. "You look less enthusiastic about the proposal."

Thabiti looked up, and back down. "Well, it happened a bit too quickly. One minute I was eating a muffin and the next, Pearl and I will be joining Marina to tend to the wishes of an overprivileged and filthy rich family in their new safari lodge."

Marina stiffened and glowered at Thabiti. "If that's how you really feel, why didn't you have the guts to tell Ollie?

Now I'll have to go back and say to him that you don't want to go, and I might lose the opportunity." She groaned. "And that means I'll have to return home with my family so Da can introduce me to a 'nice Indian man'."

Thabiti pinched his nose and closed his eyes. "I told you. I find it really hard being around strange people. If they start telling me what to do, or they get annoyed with me, I know I'll just shrink into my shell and be of little use to anyone."

Rose squeezed Thabiti's shoulder. "You're going to have to learn to stand up for yourself. Your mother isn't here anymore to shelter you from the world, and you have Pearl to protect. Besides, this will be a great opportunity for you to gain some independence, and consider what you want to do with your life. I think learning how to deal with people in small doses is a good idea and, Marina, you'll do most of the of the face-to-face work, won't you?"

Marina nodded enthusiastically. "Exactly. Ollie mainly wants you there to deal with all the new electrical equipment. I wouldn't have a clue where to start." She patted his arm. "Look, I really do appreciate you helping me out, and besides, who knows, it might be fun. Just think of all those safaris we can go on."

"Did someone mention safari?" Chloe appeared and stood next to Rose.

Rose turned to Chloe and tilted her head. "I'm sorry I left you. Have you been OK?"

"Yes, perfectly. Frank's wife Wendy found me and asked if I could help double-check some guard post checklists. The scoring's far more complicated than I realised. Anyway, there's a bit more time to get it sorted since the results and prize-giving have been delayed until half past nine tomorrow morning."

Marina sat up. "Have they? Why have they done that?"

Sam's tone was sombre. "As a mark of respect for Mayur."

Rose added, "And to prevent the winning teams celebrating loudly and drunkenly tonight."

"Has anyone seen or spoken to Jono?" Chloe clutched her bag to her chest. "Marina told me her Uncle Deepak was behind the sabotage, but that it was actually Jono who did the damage. I know he shouldn't have, but I do hope he won't be arrested again. Not after all he's been through."

Rose glanced across at Sam, took a deep breath, and said, "The situation has changed."

CHAPTER FORTY-FOUR

Rose, Sam, Chloe, Thabiti, and Marina huddled around a small circular table as Sam explained, "The results of the autopsy revealed that Mayur did not die as a result of his injuries from the car crash. He was suffocated."

Chloe crossed her arms. "Where? In the medical tent?"

Rose leant back. "I presume so."

Sam turned to her. "Mama Rose, what did you see this morning when you entered the tent? Was the zip fastened?"

Rose thought back. Her early morning visit seemed a lifetime ago. Closing her eyes, she tried to recall each step. "The tent flap was open, so I held it back and peered inside. There were two beds and the one on the right was unoccupied and in disarray. I noticed a glass of water had been knocked over beside it, because there were small puddles on the floor. And a blanket had fallen from one of the beds."

"Mayur was on the second bed, on his back and only partially covered by the sheet and I could see the exposed top of his hip. I also saw that his injured arm had been strapped up, but his forearm was bruised and free of the sling. His skin had the waxy look of death and his eyes were open and bloodshot. It gave me the feeling that he fought death." Rose opened her eyes. "I didn't know he literally fought it."

Thabiti wrinkled his forehead and nodded his head from one side to the other. "How do you suffocate someone?" He looked at Sam. "Apart from using sheer strength and your own body weight."

Sam glared at Thabiti who quickly looked down.

Thinking aloud, Rose said, "If Mayur was asleep, the killer could sneak up on him and catch him unaware, and that would give them a huge advantage. He was a strong man and I watched him drive down that slope yesterday. He certainly had courage and determination. He must have fought his attacker."

Jumping in, Chloe said, "But he was injured. Not just his arm. His whole body must have ached, particularly his head and neck. And he may have been drowsy from the effect of painkillers."

"He wasn't drowsy when I overheard him shouting at Lavanya and Jono," retorted Rose.

Chloe clicked her fingers against the table edge. "You never said anything. When was that?"

"Last night while you were busy partying. I went to check on Mayur and Jono in the medical tent, but I didn't go in as I heard them yelling at each other." Rose looked at Marina and Thabiti. "I didn't want to get involved, so I followed Lavanya back to the Bandit Bush Hog's camp and found you two sitting with Kumar."

"You crafty fox," quipped Thabiti.

"Don't be rude," snapped Rose.

"But you were all coy asking after Mayur. You didn't tell us you'd visited him."

Crossing her arms, Rose said, "Well, I didn't actually see him. And I didn't want to further upset Kumar or Lavanya. Anyway, he wasn't drowsy then. And I doubt he was later when he shouted at Lavanya again for bringing supper for him and Jono. Jono told me that's the reason he left the medical tent last night."

Chloe leant back, lacing her fingers together on her lap. "Here I was thinking he'd slipped peacefully into unconsciousness, when in reality he spent the evening winding himself and others up, and getting himself murdered."

Thabiti's brow was still wrinkled. "But how? I don't understand how he was suffocated."

Sam gave Thabiti a pitying look. "Someone of my size could have leant on him as he was lying down and pushed the air out of his lungs."

Thabiti added quickly, "And probably crushed a few ribs."

Sam growled and Thabiti hastily pushed his chair back.

"Can I continue?" Sam raised his eyebrows at Thabiti who slowly nodded. "Leaning on Mayur to remove the air from his lungs would not be enough, though. I would also have to close his airways by sealing his mouth and nose."

Marina leant forward. "How would you do that?"

Sam took her right hand and held it up against his huge hand. "I could probably use my hand to cover both his nose and mouth, but yours is too small. You would need one to cover his mouth and one to pinch his nose."

Marina cried, "But even if he was drugged, he was bound to wake up if I did that."

"I agree." Sam nodded slowly. "He would have struggled and thrashed around. You would soon lose your grip."

Politely, Thabiti asked, "So how else could it have been done?"

"With a pillow," announced Rose. "The one I spotted thrown on top of the empty bed."

"It wouldn't be quick," stated Sam.

164

Rose nodded. "It would take several minutes. The brain utilises twenty percent of the body's oxygen, so when the air supply is cut off, it soon stops functioning. But the heart continues beating even after the brain is irreversibly damaged. The killer must have been very determined, as the process could have taken as long as five minutes."

"It would be quicker if they used duct tape," Chloe declared. "I watched a programme where it was used to seal the mouth and nose. Much easier and cleaner."

Rose conceded, "I haven't seen the medical officer's findings or his report, so I've no idea if there are remnants of duct tape on his mouth."

Thabiti bit his lip. "Surely someone would have heard him struggling. What about the medics? Didn't they check on him?"

"I'm not sure. I think that's where we should start, Sam," suggested Rose.

"Start what?" Thabiti frowned. "If you become embroiled in another murder case, Craig will kill me. He told me to keep an eye on you."

Marina turned to Thabiti and slapped his thigh. "Oh, I'm sure she'll be OK. After all, she has us to help her. Don't you. Rose?"

Pink spots appeared on Thabiti's cheeks.

Rose leant forward and covered his hand with hers. "I'm just trying to help Kumar find some answers and justice for his son. The police won't arrive until tomorrow, when everyone will be getting ready to leave. Nick West is concerned they will try and pin the murder on the easiest target, and that could be you, Thabiti."

Marina put a hand around Thabiti's shoulders and drew him to her. "We all need a break. Let's go on a game drive. I've commandeered a car." She shook Ollie's car keys in the air.

Chloe clasped her hands together. "About time. Why don't I get some food and drinks for sundowners. Who wants to help?"

Rose turned to Sam. "I do think we need to speak to the medics. They may even have left."

Sam nodded.

"What time is it?" Rose asked.

"Half past three," responded Thabiti, checking his watch.

Rose said, "Shall we meet up in an hour? Give us all time to get organised. Chloe, can you fetch a jumper and my fleece jacket from the tent?"

"Chloe, I'll help you with the food and drink," offered Thabiti.

Marina stood. "I need to get changed and check my camp to make sure nobody else has been murdered. I'll meet you all at four-thirty at the entrance to headquarters. Look for a tan-coloured, long wheelbase safari vehicle with a canvas roof, and 'Kifaru Safaris' and a Rhino head logo on the side."

CHAPTER FORTY-FIVE

S am and Rose arrived at the medical tent to find both ends tied open so air could pass through and cleanse the interior. As Rose suspected, the tent had been cleared and cleaned, with the beds stripped down and the floor washed. Two thin blue mattresses lay across the bonnet and roof of a rusty, white 4x4 car with Amref printed on the side.

Rose found the paramedic who'd examined Mayur's body in the morning packing plastic boxes into the back of the 4x4.

"Hello again," she said, but was met with a blank look. "We met this morning when you confirmed that Mayur Chauhan was dead."

"Of course." The paramedic lifted another box into the vehicle.

"Are you leaving tonight?" she asked.

"No, first thing in the morning. It will take us at least six hours to get to Nairobi in this old vehicle."

"Did you hear that the patient died from suffocation, and not as a result of his injuries from the car crash?"

The paramedic stopped his work. "Well, I know nothing about that. Did he have sleep apnea? Nobody told us if he did."

Sam pulled at his throat. "What's sleep apnea?"

The paramedic pushed a plastic box to the far end of the car's boot. "It's a sleeping disorder where the patient repeatedly stops and restarts breathing. It's more common than you think."

Rose tapped her fingers together. "Usually the actual cause of death from that is a heart attack, but the medical examiner didn't say anything. When did members of your team check on Mayur?"

"My colleague checked on both patients at eight o'clock before we went to supper. She heard them shouting at each other. I looked in when we returned, but it was quite late, around midnight. Mr Urquhart must have discharged himself, as his bed was empty, and Mr Chauhan appeared to be asleep, so I didn't disturb him. I didn't visit again until you called me this morning."

She asked, "Did you all go to supper?"

"Yes, we were given vouchers to eat at the Rusty Nail. Yesterday was tiring, so after supper we relaxed and watched the antics of the competitors and spectators. I had to treat someone's hand after they'd cut it on a broken Tusker bottle."

Rose was annoyed by the apparent lack of concern for a dead patient who had been in his care. "So nobody checked if he was alive after eight pm, and he could have been dead when you looked in at midnight? You didn't actually check if he was breathing?"

The paramedic stepped back and twisted his head. "We did our job. And it was hard work yesterday. We had no reason to closely monitor the patient, as he was full of life and shouting at his wife or Mr Urquhart most of the evening. To be honest, we were relieved he was sleeping peacefully."

Rose spotted Jono peering into the tent from the far side. "Hi," she called. "Are you looking for something?"

Jono scratched his jaw, "I was just looking for... my team top. I thought I left it here."

"I'm sorry," said the paramedic. "We didn't see it when we cleaned the tent earlier."

What had he really been looking for, Rose wondered. There was much she had to discuss with Jono. He now knew he had not directly caused Mayur's death, although he may have contributed to it. Mayur was only in the medical tent because of the accident. So had that been the opportunity the killer needed?

Rose also had the nagging feeling that Jono's return had triggered more than just sabotaging a car.

"Jono," she called, "I've noticed you've been under the weather recently. Why not join us? We're going on a safari shortly, and a trip away from camp might do you good."

Jono's eyes darted from left to right. "I don't think I can, I..."

"Nonsense," interrupted the paramedic. "I doubt you slept a wink last night looking at the state of you. You're stressed out. Take this as your doctor's orders. Go on a nice long drive, see some nature and reconnect with the world."

"OK," he replied in a toneless voice. He dropped his chin to his chest.

CHAPTER FORTY-SIX

R ose and Sam wandered back through the centre of the
headquarters. Three 4x4 vehicles passed them,
jammed with people. Children rode on the roof racks of two
of the cars, dangling their legs over the edge, whilst a blonde-
haired girl poked her head out of the sunroof of the third car.

Sam commented, "It looks like we're not the only ones
heading into the Mara this evening."

Rose spotted Chloe and Thabiti standing by a long
wheelbase Land Cruiser safari vehicle. Three rows of rear
seats were covered by a canvas roof to provide welcome
shade, whilst the rolled-up sides enabled maximum game
viewing.

Rose observed, "This looks rather cumbersome to drive. I
hope Marina can handle it."

"Don't worry." Marina arrived at the vehicle panting.
"I've driven it before. All aboard."

"Sam, why don't you sit in the front next to Marina? I bet
you're an excellent animal spotter." Sam did as Rose
suggested.

"Thabiti and Chloe, you take the first row of seats. Jono
and I'll keep out of the way at the back."

Chloe whispered, "It's not like you to organise the seating arrangements. What are you up to?"

"Wait and see," responded Rose.

Chloe climbed up into the vehicle. Thabiti lifted her cool box through the open door and slid it along the floor.

Marina grated the gears, "Sorry," she called as they slowly manoeuvred out of headquarters into the Maasai Mara. "We'll head northeast across the plains to the Olare Orok River."

The car turned right and climbed over a small hill. The valley beyond consisted of patches of short yellow grass interspersed with dusty brown areas. Rose observed Maasai herdsmen, wrapped in red shukas, leaning on their long sticks. They watched their herds of cream and brown cattle, which had large humps at the base of their necks, nibble at short blades of grass.

"Rose," Marina shouted so she could be heard at the back of the vehicle. "Mara North does get overrun with cattle, but they've tried to restrict it, by introducing a managed rotational grazing programme. Don't worry everyone, we'll be out of the current grazing area shortly."

The track cut between two hills and a vast expanse of long green grass opened up before them. A herd of zebra munched peacefully to their left beside three inquisitive giraffes. Sam turned to the rear passengers. "The zebra are smart. They know giraffes, with their long necks, can easily spot danger which they cannot. You will often see groups of zebra and giraffes together."

"Why are those funny antelope standing on top of small mounds?" Chloe pointed to large deer-like animals with glossy brick-coloured coats, long faces, and straight ridged horns which turned in at the top.

"Those are topi. They love to stand sentry on termite mounds and survey the surrounding area." They drove towards distant trees as clumps of bushes began to break up the grassland. "Keep quiet," whispered Sam. "See these broken branches? There are elephants around."

Rose spotted the dark grey wrinkled hind quarters of an adolescent elephant. Marina stopped the car, but kept the engine running. Rose knew it was to enable a quick getaway, forwards or in reverse, should they need it.

"Oh," cooed Chloe, lifting up a long-lensed camera. A large elephant stepped out of the bushes and crossed the road in front of them, followed unhurriedly by other elephants of various sizes. There were a couple of baby elephants within the herd. Marina drove forward and they watched the retreating bottoms of the elephant stragglers.

Chloe leaned out of the vehicle and called, "For large animals, they move really quickly."

The track wound its way between denser vegetation.

"Stop," called Thabiti. "Reverse."

Marina followed his instructions.

"Stop. Yes, I was right. Look at that hyena." Thabiti pointed to their left.

Rose gasped and had to stop herself laughing. She had been on many game drives, but wild animals still surprised and delighted her. Less than two metres away, in the bushes, a hyena watched them from the safety of its den: a hole with built-up dirt sides. Two younger members of the family popped their heads up before all three disappeared. Rose shook her head, wondering if she had imagined the scene.

"Well spotted," Chloe cried as she turned her camera round so the viewing panel faced Thabiti. "Look, I've a great shot of it staring straight into the lens."

"That's not something you see every day," Sam chuckled.

CHAPTER FORTY-SEVEN

M arina drove the heavy Land Cruiser along the banks of the Olare Orok River as they searched for an elusive leopard. In the end they were content to just sit and watch the antics of a family of baboons preparing for the night ahead. Marina took a different route back towards headquarters, and parked under an acacia tree as day gave way to dusk.

She turned off the ignition and announced to her passengers, "This is a great place to watch the sunset."

Marina removed a small table from the back of the car and arranged a shuka blanket over it. Sam pulled Chloe's cool box from the vehicle and placed it beside the table. Thabiti and Chloe scrambled out of the back.

Beside Rose, Jono had been silent during the game drive, but he had begun to take an interest in the animals they spotted. He prepared to stand, but Rose placed a hand on his thigh. "There's something I need to discuss with you before we join the others."

Jono flinched and his eyes were as wary as any animal they'd seen on their safari.

She began, "I've been told about the car accident, the one that happened twenty years ago."

Jono closed his eyes and clenched his hand.

"Marina outlined the events and her cousin Aatma filled in the details. Is the crash the reason you've been away from your home, and from Kenya, for so long?"

Jono nodded.

"Do you mind telling me what you remember about the accident?"

Jono looked at her with wide, haunted eyes. "Mind, how can I mind?" He slowly shook his head. "I don't remember anything. Nothing from the day before the crash until I woke up in hospital three days later. The doctors told me I was lucky to be alive, but I wanted to die. Vadhana was dead. And she was such a lively, vivacious girl."

She wished she could help alleviate his pain. She said in a soothing voice, "How did you find out about the crash?"

Jono tugged at the collar of his polo shirt and replied, "From the police when they arrested me."

"What about Aatma, did he visit you in hospital?"

Jono shook his head. "He was too angry to visit me. I heard he flew home with Vadhana's body, and I didn't see or speak to him again." Jono wiped the back of his hand across his cheek.

Marina returned to the car for a basket, but she didn't look at them and hurried back to the table.

Rose continued to probe. "And have you seen or spoken to him since you've been back in Kenya?"

Jono looked up at her and responded, "No. I think I saw him in Nairobi once, but he disappeared before I could speak to him."

She placed her hands on her thighs and stated, "But you have spoken with Deepak Seth."

Jono shuffled in his seat and averted his gaze. "He

cornered me at Wilson Airport, after I flew some tourists down from Nanyuki. I couldn't just ignore him."

She decided it was time to get to the point. "Did he blackmail you to make sure Kumar Chauhan's team didn't beat his at this year's Rhino Charge?"

Jono stiffened. "Why would he want to do that?"

"Because of his rivalry and resentment towards Kumar, and he's fed up with being beaten by him. And before Kumar was injured, he would have been driving."

Jono crossed his arms. "Why do you think I did anything? Who tampered with the car's engine? And who hid the safety equipment?"

She wrinkled her nose. "I thought you had. Are you telling me you didn't?"

Jono opened his arms. "I swear, I had nothing to do with those incidents."

She repeated his response in her mind, rubbed her ear, and asserted, "But you did pretend to lose the sponsor's cheque?"

Jono drooped. "I thought that if the Bandit Bush Hogs couldn't meet their entry pledge they wouldn't be able to take part. It was the simplest way to stop them beating the Rhino Force team."

Chloe's laughter reached them.

Rose said, "Losing a cheque is one thing, but interfering with winch equipment is quite another. Why did you do it?"

Jono held up his hands. "Please believe me, I never meant to hurt Mayur. But I was desperate. And I didn't know what else to do. When I used to attend Rhino Charges, years ago as a teenager, the drivers never attempted to descend such steep slopes. When Mayur explained the route he wanted to take, I tried to persuade him to find an easier alternative, but he was insistent. Perhaps he needed to show everyone he was as good a driver as his father."

"But you didn't stop him. And you haven't owned up

about what you did." Rose wanted to be sympathetic, but she knew her words sounded harsh.

Jono didn't appear to notice, but gently rocked to and fro. "He refused to listen and I was frantic. But the team backed him and I had to watch every inch of his descent, praying the winch strop would hold. Unlike last time, I can remember every detail, and it keeps playing round and round in my head."

Rose still didn't feel very sympathetic. "And what did you do when you heard that Mayur had died?"

Jono was shaking and his voice was unsteady as he said, "I went to Deepak, but he refused to accept any responsibility. He told me it was my all fault, as I decided to interfere with the winch equipment. I suppose he felt justified that this time I remembered the crash and could feel the pain of the damage I'd caused."

Jono looked out at the orange sky. "I'm a coward. I should have confessed straight away, but I just couldn't. And then everyone started blaming Thabiti. And you and Sam, all of you, were so united searching for the truth. I resented such teamwork, as nobody supported me twenty years ago. My father sent me away to a sheep farm in the north of Scotland and barely spoke to me again."

Jono shuffled his feet. "But I had made up my mind this afternoon, and I was going to tell you everything. And then you announced Mayur had been suffocated. I was utterly confused."

Rose decided Jono needed a break from her interrogation, but she knew she'd have to finish what she'd started. "Let's get out and stretch our legs. I'm sure Chloe brought some Tuskers."

Thabiti and Marina were eating crisps from a bowl on the small table, and Chloe was standing behind them taking photographs of the sunset.

As Rose climbed down from the car, she spotted Sam reaching into the cool box and shouted to him, "Can you bring Jono a Tusker? And is there any white wine?" Sam held up a bottle. "Please can you pour me a small glass?"

Rose and Jono stood apart from the others, standing side by side, watching the sunset.

Rose said, "I cannot excuse you for what you did. Your actions caused a horrendous accident and you let an innocent boy take the blame. But I now know Deepak's been planning a way to beat Kumar's team for a while."

Jono ran a hand through his unruly hair. "I don't understand. What has he been planning?"

Rose turned to Jono and said, "Did Deepak tell you to ask Kumar if you could relocate the car to a garage in Nanyuki?"

"Yes, he did. And Kumar agreed, as the team's usual mechanic couldn't make it back for the Charge from work this year. I told Kumar I'd find him a replacement mechanic."

"Because that was what Deepak told you to say?" Jono dragged his foot though the dusty ground, and as he didn't answer, Rose continued. "Deepak has admitted he fixed it so that the usual mechanic would be working away, and that he instructed you to find someone who only had limited mechanical experience."

Sam strolled over and looked at each of them as he handed them their drinks. "OK?" he asked.

Rose nodded.

Sam returned to Marina and Thabiti, who were chatting loudly.

Jono pulled back the ring pull on his Tusker and asked. "But why would Deepak care who the mechanic was?"

Rose sipped her wine. "I guess someone with less experience would be unlikely to discover what you'd done to tamper with the car. Also, I think he wanted to watch you squirm, as you chose between admitting your guilt, and the

177

risk that someone would find out about your criminal conviction, or keeping your secret hidden and letting an innocent boy take the blame."

Jono kicked the ground. "Deepak really is devious. I should never have agreed to his plan in the first place, but I knew he could ruin any chance I had of living back here in Kenya. Of being with my old friends. Of being happy."

The sun was only half visible and an orange glow spread across the horizon.

Rose commented, "Somebody said Deepak is bitter and twisted, and they're probably right. And he will always mourn the loss of his favourite child. But I've learnt many things today which all begin with that tragic car accident so long ago." She paused. "And I suspect the motive behind Mayur's death starts there, too."

CHAPTER FORTY-EIGHT

Marina drove slowly in the evening gloom, guided by the bright glow of headquarters in the distance. Thabiti sat next to her in the front with Rose and Jono in the first row of rear seats. Chloe was huddled in her padded jacket next to Sam, behind them.

Marina shouted above the noise of the engine as the car crawled its way up a steep, rocky track. "Jono, were you at school with Mayur and my cousins?" Clearly the earlier conversations in her camp were still playing on her mind.

Jono answered, "I think Mayur asked me to join the Bandit Bush Hogs because we were at school together, although we were never really friends. I was in the year above his wife Lavanya and poor Vadhana. He and your cousin Hinesh were older, and I always remember them as the senior boys. Mayur was large and strong and played in the front row of an unbeaten senior school rugby team. And you wouldn't think to look at him now, but Hinesh was fast and played on the wing."

Jono sipped from his can of Tusker with a far-away look. "I'd forgotten how close your cousin Aatma and I were back then. I was an outcast, being a mzungu, and he was the archetypal brain box with glasses and a nervous manner. That is until he was on the running track. Do you know he broke the national schools' four hundred metres record in the lower sixth? But he wasn't always quick enough to get away from Mayur, who was a bully. Mayur ran a gang which picked on Aatma."

"Poor Aatma," called Marina. "I like him and he's always kind to me, but he is nervous and rarely joins in. He leads a solitary life."

Chloe leaned forward and addressed Jono. "Could your reappearance in Kenya have triggered those old, painful memories for Aatma? And could he have focused on Mayur who caused him so much pain and grief as a child?"

Jono shrugged his shoulders.

Chloe sat up and looked at them with bright eyes. "Mayur was injured and less able to defend himself, so Aatma might have seen it as the perfect opportunity for vengeance."

Rose replied, "I guess it is possible," but somehow she doubted it.

Sam announced, "I think what happened is down to business rivalry. Hinesh told us Mayur was running much of the business without Kumar's knowledge. And he was engaging in unscrupulous practices, such as undermining the Seths' prices in order to gain business. Hinesh told us he wouldn't mourn Mayur's death."

The entrance to headquarters loomed into sight. Rose had missed lunch and the smell of BBQ meat hung tantalisingly in the air.

She added, "Mayur suspected the confusion over orders, which prevented his brother attending the Charge, had been instigated by the Seths, but I don't see how."

No one answered.

They drove into headquarters and Marina parked. Thabiti spoke for the first time. "I smell nyama choma."

Rose said, "I wonder if anyone has told Mayur's brother about his death?"

"I'll check," replied Jono. "I need to see how poor Lavanya is doing. She has to support Kumar, organise camp, and deal with her own grief."

"Or relief," muttered Chloe.

CHAPTER FORTY-NINE

R ose and her group were unloading the safari car when they heard shouts from parc fermé. Turning, Rose spotted a figure waving a stick.

"That's Kumar," cried Thabiti. "Who's he shouting at?"

"I can't see in the gloom, and whoever's holding the light won't keep it still," replied Chloe.

"I bet it's Uncle Deepak," moaned Marina.

Marina was right as Rose heard Deepak shout, "Don't you dare go near my car."

Kumar threw his head back and cackled, "We're going to have ourselves a lovely bonfire. Lavanya, my dear, bring me that lamp."

"Oh no you don't," Deepak countered.

The lamp wavered violently and Rose heard Lavanya cry out.

Sam instructed Thabiti, "Quick, find a fire extinguisher."

Thabiti threw his arms in the air, "Where from?"

"One of the cars," Chloe answered and grabbed Thabiti's arm. "I'll help you." And they vanished into the dark.

"Marina, I might need your help." Sam strode towards the shouts, followed by Rose and Marina.

Lavanya cried, "Ow, you're hurting me."

Jono ran past.

Rose could now make out Deepak, who was being wrestled away from Lavanya by Jono. Kumar leant against the Rhino Force car and was struggling to support himself. Marina rushed across to him whilst Sam confronted Deepak.

"Let her go, Mr Seth." Sam's voice was controlled but had a steely edge. "Give me the lamp, Lavanya, and tell me what's going on."

Lavanya's quiet voice murmured, "Kumar insisted I bring him here and carry a kerosene lamp. I thought it was just to light our way."

Hinesh emerged from the darkness. "Da, what's going on?"

Deepak struggled against Jono's restraint and replied, "He's mad. He's trying to set fire to our car and who knows how many other vehicles."

Sam nodded to Jono, who let go of Deepak.

Deepak turned and swung at Jono with his fist, but Jono caught it. "You've caused enough pain and suffering. I'm very sorry for what happened to Vadhana, but that doesn't excuse you from making me damage Kumar's vehicle. We caused a terrible accident. And of course Kumar is upset. Surely you of all people should understand. His child is dead."

Hinesh held his hand out towards Deepak. "Da, you better come with me."

Deepak tugged his fist out of Jono's grasp, spat at his feet, and marched into the darkness.

Rose spoke to Jono. "Why don't you take Lavanya back to camp?" She turned to Hinesh, "Can you wait a moment?"

Thabiti and Chloe rushed forward, each holding a fire extinguisher.

"Panic over," declared Sam.

Thabiti's shoulders sagged. "Now what do we do? I'll never remember which car I grabbed this from."

"Let's leave them by the entrance," suggested Chloe. "Hopefully the right teams will spot them as they drive out."

Rose moved across to Sam and said, "Can you assist Kumar back to his camp? I want a private word with Hinesh."

She found Hinesh waiting patiently in the gloom.

He said in a tired voice, "Our past troubles continue to haunt us."

They meandered between cars and left parc fermé.

Rose asked, "Is your father on his own? I've not seen your mother here."

"This wouldn't be her thing. But she died over thirty years ago, when a lorry knocked her off the back of a boda boda. I think that's why Da concentrated his affection on Vadhana, who was the youngest, and then he lost her as well."

"Poor man. I understand it hit him deeply, so deeply that he nearly let the business collapse."

"He couldn't concentrate and kept making damaging decisions, but he refused to listen to any of us. Kumar worked hard, countering many of them, and he helped me gain a better understanding of the company, and the way things worked."

It was lighter in the centre of camp. They paused as a group of people, looking cosy in their warm jackets, walked across their path in the direction of the Rusty Nail.

Rose asked, "But then Kumar left?"

Hinesh rubbed his hands together and replied, "I don't blame him for leaving. Da was constantly angry, lashing out at us with his tongue, and at his workers… with anything that came to hand. Kumar caught him beating one of them, and that was the final straw. As I said, I don't blame Kumar for leaving, but it was setting up in competition, when he knew we were struggling, that irked me."

They walked past the beer tent. There was only the dull murmur of voices, in contrast to the animated celebrations of the previous evening.

Rose said, "How do you feel about Kumar now?"

Hinesh shrugged. "He's always polite to us, even to Da who refuses to be civil back. And I have a great deal of respect for him and what he has achieved with his company. In fairness, although he initially stole some of our clients, once he was established he targeted smaller hotels and restaurants. He left our contracts with the larger hotel chains and lodges alone."

"But earlier you were complaining Mayur was targeting your customers and undercutting you."

"Mayur was, but not Kumar, who I doubt knew anything about it. I understand he spends less time in the office and was beginning to bow to Mayur's demands for more control over the business. Still, I know he would be furious if he found out what Mayur was doing."

Rose wondered exactly what he meant. "Undercutting you, or something else?"

"Well, I heard last week that Mayur was talking with investors, as I was given the heads up by one of them. What a cheek, it's our operation he was targeting."

They entered the Rhino Force camp via the gazebo. Beside a tent, one of the children was being subjected to a bucket bath. He stood naked in a black bucket whilst his Ayah scooped mugfuls of water out of the bucket and poured them over his soapy body.

Rose remembered doing the same for Heather and Chris on a family safari when they were children. Chris usually attacked Heather when she was in the bucket, causing her to knock it over and the pair of them would run naked around the camp until Rose and their Ayah caught and bathed them both again.

"But surely Kumar wouldn't allow Mayur to target your company. I heard he was refusing to move to new premises because it was an unnecessary expense, and he was concerned about the impact on his staff."

"That's why Mayur was pushing him out and it wasn't just the business. Mayur was desperate to drive the Bandit Bush Hog's team car, but Kumar always drove and provided the majority of the sponsorship money."

"So his wish was granted when Kumar had a hockey accident and injured his foot."

Hinesh scoffed. "That was no accident. I was playing on the opposing team. I saw Mayur deliberately stamp on his father's foot, and he fractured two metatarsals."

CHAPTER FIFTY

Rose trekked back to the Bandit Bush Hog's camp, picking her way carefully in the dark until she reached the brighter central area of headquarters.

She met Chloe and Thabiti emerging from the bar. "Lavanya insisted we all stay for supper. You, too," announced Chloe. She carefully hoisted her bag over her shoulder as glass bottles clanked inside. "I volunteered to buy the drinks." They followed Thabiti who carried two six-packs of Tusker cans.

Kumar sat crumpled in his plastic chair at the head of the table with a shuka blanket draped over his shoulders. Rose sat down next to him as aromatic curry dishes were placed on the table. Kumar set his jaw and pulled himself upright in his chair. His blanket fell to the floor and was picked up by one of the camp staff.

He turned to Rose and grasped her hand. "My earlier behaviour was irrational, shameful. Please accept my apologies."

Rose whispered. "You scared Lavanya. She's the one you need to apologise to."

Lavanya was seated at the opposite end of the table,

between Thabiti and Jono. Kumar addressed her. "I'm sorry to embarrass you and force you to heed to the whims of an old man. You have done my son and myself proud providing such a feast for our guests on this sad day. Let us pray."

Rose was grateful for the warming food. She tasted a lentil curry. "Is this the same dish you took Mayur and Jono last night?" she asked Lavanya.

"Similar," responded Jono.

"It's delicious," she complimented Lavanya, who rubbed her hand against her forehead. Rose saw an angry red mark on the inside of her arm, just below her wrist.

Lavanya whipped her arm away and muttered, "Cooking accident." Rose was not so sure, but her eyesight was not great in the dull light thrown by the paraffin lamps.

With each mouthful, Kumar appeared to regain his strength and lucidity. He turned to Rose. "Have you found proof yet that Deepak killed my son?"

Rose glanced at Jono, whose skin was flushed, before responding. "Deepak was playing a different game. His energy was focused on beating your team in the Rhino Charge, and I don't believe he was involved with Mayur's death."

Kumar grunted. "More likely to be his son. I remember he was good friends with Mayur at school, but their relationship soured in adulthood."

Kumar ate another mouthful of curry.

Rose turned to Kumar. "I've just spoken to Hinesh, and he has a great respect for you. He told me you taught him to run the business when his father went off the rails after Vadhana's death."

Kumar broke off a piece of chapati. "Those were difficult times for everyone. Hinesh was not the brightest boy, but he was diligent and he did well to keep the business afloat as I doubt Deepak had much input."

Rose leant forward and spoke quietly, "So it's understandable Hinesh was annoyed when he discovered Mayur was undercutting them, and planning a takeover of his father's company."

Kumar flinched. "I wouldn't have allowed it. I know what a family business means, and the sweat and sacrifices it takes to start and grow such an enterprise. Besides, if the Seths approached me, I would consider a merger, but not a hostile takeover, however much Mayur insisted."

Rose asked, "Was Mayur very ambitious?"

Kumar shook his head and replied, "He was, but for all the wrong reasons. He thought respect and standing in the community came from owning a large house and driving the latest flash car. But of course he was wrong. People are admired for what they do and how they act, not for what they have. And I repeated this mantra many times, but he chose to ignore me. As I am beginning to think he ignored many of my instructions."

Rose touched Kumar's hand. "Were you close?"

"Not particularly, and he thought I favoured his younger brother. And perhaps I do. My now departed wife spoilt Mayur and she was wrong to encourage his grandiose plans."

Thabiti had finished his curry and was gazing greedily at Lavanya's plate as she giggled at something Jono said.

Rose turned back to Kumar, "Do you think he would deliberately harm you?"

"Don't be ridiculous. Why should he?" Kumar pushed his plate of food away. He refused to look Rose in the eye.

"Well you were standing in his way, refusing to give up control of the business and allow him to implement his expansion plans."

Kumar's eyebrows gathered together. "But he is the one who died, not me."

Rose decided to change tack. "Was this the first year he had driven the team's car?"

Kumar leaned back. "I've always driven, since we began ten years ago. It was an ambition of mine and one of my few vices. So I worked hard and I funded the team with my own money, not the company's. I loved it, although I will admit I am not as brave as other drivers these days. Perhaps Mayur was right to insist he drive. I heard the slope he attempted was very steep. I would have taken an alternative route."

Marina handed Thabiti the rice and curry dishes. He spooned their remaining contents onto his plate.

Rose placed her knife and fork on the table and locked eyes with Kumar. "I have to ask you again, would Mayur deliberately hurt you to achieve his desires?"

Kumar's eyes were wide, unblinking and haunted. "I, I…" he stammered.

Rose placed her hand on Kumar's arm. "It's OK. Hinesh told me about the hockey accident. He saw it happen."

Kumar gulped. "The Seths were on the opposition. And Mayur insisted one of them stamped on my foot and I believed him…" Kumar grasped Rose's hand. "I knew it was Mayur, but I refused to believe, to accept it. I should have stood up to him."

Marina and Chloe began collecting the empty plates. Rose ignored her own unfinished one as she held Kumar's tormented gaze. He was quivering. Rose sensed there was more. "So you paid him back?"

The words gushed out. "I know I shouldn't have. It was sinful." Kumar gulped again. "When the camp was empty, and Lavanya was resting, I opened the car bonnet. I leant against the car for support and only meant to check the engine, but a wickedness overcame me. I unhooked the electrical connectors to prevent the car from starting and hid the damage under the spark plug cover.

Thabiti is a nice boy, but he's not a qualified mechanic. And I thought my actions would delay, or even prevent the team completing the scrutineering, which would send Mayur into a rage, and pay him back."

"But it didn't." Rose's words were soft and soothing.

"No." Kumar jerked upright. "There was all the commotion about missing safety equipment. And when it was discovered and the team was ready to leave, instead of failing to start, the car purred into life. It was only later that I overheard Sam and Thabiti. They were cataloguing a sequence of occurrences they had discovered aimed at sabotaging the team's chances of competing. The engine was one of them.

I hadn't meant Thabiti to get into trouble, but I'm afraid I didn't own up." Kumar hung his head, brought his hands together, and Rose watched his lips move. She allowed him to finish his prayer.

The camp staff placed two bowls of small round sticky donuts on the table. Thabiti rubbed his hands together as he eyed them.

Kumar continued, "I visited him, Mayur, in the medical tent with Lavanya's help. He might have been injured, but his temper was undiminished. He was furious about the accident, and not about his health, but because it allowed the Seths to beat him. I think his ego was severely dented. And he told me we had to go ahead with his plans to buy out the Seths as payback for what they had done. Never mind his injuries, I thought he would have a heart attack. He was red in the face and puffing. He shouted insults at Lavanya who ran out of the tent. I found her sitting under the shade of a tree being consoled by Aatma Seth."

Rose thought out loud, "I wonder what he was doing there?"

"I've no idea. Jono was also in the medical tent and he

chastised Mayur, and told him to hold his tongue. But he received a torrent of abuse for his trouble. I actually thought Jono was going to jump out of bed and throttle Mayur where he lay."

Kumar hung his head again. "That was the first time I was truly ashamed of my son, and it was the last time I saw him." Kumar sighed and shook his head. "I will end my years a lonely old man for my failings."

Rose leant forward. "You have another son and a daughter-in-law who dotes on you." Kumar looked along the table at Lavanya. Her face glowed under the attention of Thabiti and Jono. "She is young with her life in front of her. She should not stay a widow. But she needs to marry a man who loves her."

CHAPTER FIFTY-ONE

After supper, Kumar made his excuses and Lavanya assisted him to his tent. Marina, Chloe, and Thabiti settled themselves into the folding camp chairs by the fire pit.

Rose turned to Sam, who had remained seated at the table, and said, "You were very quiet during supper. Are you tired? It's been a long couple of days."

Sam smiled slowly. "Someone once told me we have two ears and one mouth and we should remember to use them in that ratio. Besides, I learn a lot when I sit quietly and observe people."

Rose tilted her head and remarked, "I must say, for your size you have an unerring habit of fading into the background. And I've noticed that people sometimes forget you're there. It's not a skill I've ever developed, but it must have its uses, particularly in your line of business."

Sam nodded and wrinkled his lips, almost in amusement, she thought.

She sat up and placed her hands on the table. "I would love to go back to my tent and just curl up in bed, but I really need to talk to the Seths again. And I hope this is the last time. I wondered if you would come with me?"

"Of course. I'm at your disposal."

Rose watched Sam as they stood. He appeared relaxed, but during supper she'd noticed him occasionally tilt his head, as if he'd heard an unusual sound, or wrinkle his nose as if detecting a scent. He reminded her of an African buffalo which had poor eyesight, but keen hearing and excellent smell which warned it of approaching predators.

She hurried to catch up with his purposeful stride and was relieved to have his reassuring presence this evening. They left the camp through the leleshwa bushes without disturbing those around the fire pit.

"Do you want to speak to Deepak again?" Sam asked as he guided her around a broken bottle.

"Not yet. It's quiet cousin Aatma I want to speak to first."

As they stepped into the gazebo at the entrance to the Seths' camp, they were once again confronted by Marina's indignant cousin, Elaxi. "Where is that girl? Have you brought her back with you?"

Rose stood straighter. She'd had enough of this woman throwing her weight around.

Sam stepped forward. "No. Marina is relaxing with her friends. She's eaten supper and will return in her own time."

"Why do I bother organising meals for her?" Elaxi flounced away.

Rose heard Deepak shout, "Not you again. What do you want now?"

She and Sam stepped into the light thrown by several solar lamps suspended from poles in the central marquee. "We'd like to speak to Aatma."

Deepak spat. "He'll be round the back smoking. Aatma," he shouted.

Aatma appeared in a pool of light at the side of the tent, holding a cigarette in one hand and a bottle of Tusker beer in the other. "Yes, Da?"

"That woman's here to speak to you again. Sit here. I'm going to use the facilities." Deepak stalked away.

Rose and Aatma sat down and Sam lowered himself carefully into a wooden safari chair.

As it was nearly nine o'clock and she was getting tired, Rose drove straight to the point. "We've just finished supper with Kumar Chauhan who told me you were hanging around outside the medical tent yesterday evening. And I also found a number of cigarettes butts beside a tree. Did you go there to check up on Mayur?"

Aatma removed his glasses. "Mayur? No, I went to see Jono."

Rose did a double take. "Oh, but I thought you were weren't talking to him?"

Aatma rubbed his eyes. "I wasn't, but then there was the crash. I just needed to see him again, that's all."

"Why?" asked Sam.

Aatma jumped up and lit another cigarette. "There's something you don't know. In fact, nobody knows but me."

They waited in expectant silence and Rose noted Sam's nose wrinkling and realised he'd caught a scent, but this time he looked like a predator.

Sam's eyes bored into Aatma and he said, "Is it something to do with yesterday's crash? Or with Mayur's death?"

Aatma turned and stared at them with wide, frightened eyes. "No, it's nothing to do with Mayur's death. Or yesterday's crash. It's about the original crash, with me and Jono and… Vadhana."

She watched him pace to and fro. He spoke as he walked.

"You see, I needed to find out how much Jono remembered. I can't believe that after all this time he still has no memory of that day."

Rose asked, "Why does it matter? And why torment yourself? It's clear it was an accident, and Jono didn't deliberately crash his car. He just got it wrong in the poor weather conditions."

One of the children in the camp shouted, "No, I'm not going to bed yet."

Aatma stood still but he didn't look at them. "That's what he believes. And what the police believe, but it's all a lie. One miserable lie which has been compounded and caused so much heartache and distress."

"Sit down," Rose commanded. "All this moving around. I can't make sense of what you're saying." She sighed, feeling weary, and her brain was beginning to fog.

"I think what he's trying to tell us, in his roundabout way," Sam scowled, "is that he had something to do with the original crash. Am I right?"

Aatma looked at the floor. "Yes."

Rose felt her head clear. "Did you cause the crash? Were you driving and not Jono?" Did he pull Jono from the car? To cover up the fact that he was driving?

Aatma breathed out heavily and sank into a chair. "Thank you. I've never been able to say the words. They've eaten away at me for twenty years, but I couldn't rid myself of them."

Rose leaned forward. "But the police said Jono was driving. Is that what you told them?"

Aatma raised his shoulders. "Not exactly. When they appeared at the scene and asked who owned the car, I told them it was Jono's. We were both on the ground outside and Jono was badly injured, so they presumed he'd been driving. I know I should have told them, or said something the next day when they questioned me, but I was a coward. I let Jono take the blame."

"Why didn't you confess later?" Sam asked.

Aatma rubbed his wrist. "I did tell Jono, but he was

unconscious. And by the time he woke up I was flying back to Kenya with Vadhana's body."

"I knew it!" exclaimed Deepak, stepping into the light.

Aatma cowered in his chair.

"How?" countered Rose.

Deepak screwed up his eyes. "He refused to tell me what really happened. And wouldn't admit what he'd done, but I knew." Deepak gulped and wailed, "He killed my beloved Vadhana."

Rose was tired. She'd had enough. "Did you actually know? Or did you just want to punish your son because he was the reason your daughter was in the car that day?"

Deepak looked at her and shook his head. "Vadhana insisted, against my better judgement, on visiting him in the UK. But I did know because he called out in his sleep. And he didn't have the guts to tell me himself."

"What?" shouted Aatma sitting up straight in his chair. "You knew, yet you still let me suffer all this time?"

"You betrayed me," cried Deepak.

Hinesh appeared in the tent. "What's happening? Why's everyone shouting?"

Sam stood, raised his arms, and said calmly, "Aatma has just admitted that he was driving the car which killed your sister. And it appears your father knew this, but he's allowed Aatma to wallow alone in his guilt."

Hinesh looked from Aatma, once more slumped in his chair, to his father, standing defiant with his arms crossed tightly over his chest. "But why now? And why here?"

Rose looked up and explained, "Everything comes back to Jono's reappearance in Kenya. It's his recent arrival which has triggered all these events."

Hinesh clasped his hands together. "But Da, you blackmailed Jono and caused Mayur's dreadful accident. Why would you do that if you knew Jono wasn't to blame?"

Deepak pinched his mouth. "I knew. But it was clear he didn't. He still remembers nothing about the crash, so I solicited his help to finally beat Kumar's team."

Hinesh shook his head. "But Da, that's cruel." He looked at Aatma who was curled up. "And so's not admitting to Aatma that you knew the truth. You've bullied him all his life."

Rose stood. "You need to sort out your own family troubles, but Jono deserves to know the truth. Best do it now, Aatma." Aatma shrank back.

"Come on." Sam lifted him out of the chair onto unsteady feet and propelled him out of the camp.

CHAPTER FIFTY-TWO

S am held Aatma by the arm as he led him out of the
Rhino Charge camp towards the Bandit Bush Hog's
camp. As they once again passed through the brightly lit
central catering area of the headquarters, Aatma stopped and
twisted out of Sam's grasp. He looked from Sam to Rose, and
asked, "Can I have a stiff drink before I confront Jono?"

Rose nodded at Sam. "All right."

Aatma gave him a thousand bob note and stated, "A
whisky."

Sam ducked inside the bar tent.

Aatma twisted his hands and then looked at Rose with
large pleading eyes. "I really am sorry for all the grief I
caused Da and Jono."

Rose placed her hand on his arm and responded, "Where
your father is concerned, I'm not sure he would have forgiven
you whatever you said or did. In fact, it was probably much
easier for him to vent his grief by bullying you, and believe
he was justified in doing so. But secrets like this are best if
they are not left buried in the past."

Sam returned with a plastic glass containing an amber

liquid. Aatma drained it. He crumpled the glass, squared his shoulders and announced, "I'm ready."

They passed small groups of people gathered around tables in the catering area and walked on into the gloom. They found the entrance for the Bandit Bush Hog's camp, between the leleshwa bushes, and entered.

There were faint pools of light outside each tent where a paraffin lamp had been positioned but the main light source was the glow of the fire pit around which Rose saw shadows and heard the mutter of voices.

She put her arms out and turned to Sam and Aatma. "I'll go and find Jono. You two wait here."

She joined the group around the fire pit. Chloe and Marina were laughing at Thabiti's confused expression, and Jono and Lavanya were whispering, their heads close together. She coughed and everyone looked up.

"Hi," exclaimed Chloe. "Wine?" she held up a bottle.

"In a minute. Jono, sorry to disturb you, but there's someone who needs to speak to you."

Jono glanced around the group. "Who?"

"It's a private matter. Can you come with me?"

Jono hesitated and looked at Lavanya as he slowly pushed himself out of his chair.

Rose tried to reassure him. "I promise I'm not trying to trick you."

In the darkness, it was difficult to make out Sam and Aatma, so she asked, "Which is your tent?"

Jono pointed.

"Over here," she called into the blackness. She and Jono stood in the small pool of lamplight, waiting for Sam and Aatma to join them.

Rose turned to Jono and laid a hand on his arm. "Aatma has something to tell you."

Aatma began to stutter, "I.."

Sam pulled Rose away. "This is one conversation you shouldn't listen to." They joined the others around the fire pit.

"Where's Jono?" Lavanya pulled at a red and green shawl wrapped over her head and shoulders.

"Catching up with an old friend," Rose replied.

Lavanya stood and took a step back. "I think I should check on Kumar."

As her figure retreated, Chloe handed Rose a glass of wine and asked, "What was that about?"

Rose turned to Sam and asked, "Can you tell them?"

Sam opened a can of Tusker, drank deeply, and began.

When he had finished his sad tale, Chloe whispered, "I've felt sorry for Jono all weekend, even though he caused the crash. And now, well it's so unfair. How could Deepak be so cruel?"

"Time and practice," remarked Marina.

"I'll second that," a voice spoke in the dark. Marina's cousin Hinesh emerged into the light thrown by the fire pit.

Hinesh asked, "Where's Aatma? I thought he might need some moral support. I'm afraid I've given him precious little in the past."

"He's still with Jono," explained Rose. "Why not wait with us? There are plenty of chairs in the events shelter."

"It's OK. I'll stand."

Hinesh gazed into the fire as if mesmerised. "When Ma was still alive we used to roast marshmallows over a fire, but Da stopped us after Vadhana burnt her lip." He looked around the group. "So is this the murder committee? I see you've joined their ranks, Marina."

Mariana quipped, "It's better than looking after cousin Elaxi's kids."

Hinesh laughed. "Elaxi may be bossy, but who can blame her? As well as her husband and their children, she has her father and us brothers to attend to." He leaned forward with an eager expression on his face. "So, who are your prime suspects?"

Rose waved smoke away from her face and coughed, "You and Aatma, for starters."

Hinesh exclaimed, "Is everything to be blamed on my family?"

She responded, "Well, Mayur was undermining your business and seeking investors to take it over."

Hinesh pulled at his chin. "He was but he didn't know that I've been having talks with his younger brother about merging the businesses. You see working together makes sense as our clients are mostly large hotel chains and lodges, whilst the Chauhans serve smaller hotels and restaurants. Through a merger we could save costs in the supply chain, and achieve economies of scale in our sales."

Rose asked, "Could Mayur have prevented your merger working?"

Hinesh turned to her. "He would certainly have tried, but his brother told me Kumar still has authority to make the important business decisions."

"So there was no reason to kill him?"

Hinesh sighed. "Kumar will decide if the merger goes ahead. Life will certainly be easier for all of us without Mayur, but in the end, Kumar was usually able to control him."

"Except when he broke his foot," she suggested.

"That was really nasty. Maybe Mayur tried to do the same to someone else and paid the price," responded Hinesh.

Thabiti leant forward and whispered, "Could Kumar have killed Mayur for causing all this trouble, and for deliberately injuring him?"

Sam answered. "I'd have said it was more likely to have been the other way around, and that Mayur benefited from getting his father out of the way."

Chloe tapped the ends of her fingers together and said, "But I can't see how Kumar could have done it. If he'd wanted to kill Mayur, it would have been much simpler to crack him over the head with a crutch. He wouldn't have been able to suffocate him."

Aatma appeared, looked at Hinesh, and said, "I thought I heard your voice. Do you fancy a drink at the bar? I need something stronger than beer."

Hinesh turned back to the group by the fire. "I hope that clarifies matters. And clears us as potential suspects." He followed his brother into the night.

CHAPTER FIFTY-THREE

T habiti stood and collected broken branches from a small pile behind his chair. He threw them on top of the fire. Headquarters was quiet with only an occasional cry or peal of laughter. Rose heard the faint roar of a lion from the Mara and an answering call.

Thabiti bit his lip and asked, "So who did kill Mayur?"

"Good question." Rose looked at Sam. "We're really no further forward are we?"

"I disagree." He placed his can in a holder in the arm of his camping chair and stretched. "At least we got to the bottom of the original car accident, which is a relief, as it's been hanging over this entire event. So now we can concentrate on the here and now. Let me ask, why do you think someone would commit a murder?"

"Love," exclaimed Chloe.

"Or hate," suggested Thabiti.

"Money. That's a prime reason." Marina rubbed her hands together as if imitating greed. "As is power and control, as my family has shown."

Rose murmured, "And jealousy."

Sam looked around the group and repeated, "Money,

power and control. Well, we know Mayur wanted all of these, but from the recent discussion with Hinesh, I don't see how anyone else would gain them from his death."

"I agree," said Rose. "I think we've exhausted motives for the Seth family. Of course, something else might turn up."

Sam arched his back. "I thought the reason lay in their businesses. But while there appears to be plenty of animosity and clashing personalities on the outside, behind the scenes their relationship seems to be cordial. So much so that they're considering an amicable merger."

Marina tapped her foot on the ground and said, "In which case Mayur would be the loser. And there was no reason for my family to get rid of him."

"Succinctly put, Marina. So where are we now?" asked Rose.

The fire spat as the fresh green wood began to burn.

'Love," voiced Chloe again.

Marina crossed her ankles. "I'm not sure anyone truly loved Mayur, apart from his mother, but she's dead now, isn't she Rose?"

Rose nodded. "She is and Kumar told me she spoilt Mayur."

"So that leaves hate," repeated Thabiti. "And I think a lot of people fall into that category."

Rose leaned towards Thabiti and said, "Possibly, but hate is a strong emotion. Most of those who disliked Mayur found a way to work round, or even without him."

Chloe linked her fingers together and rested her chin on them. "Except poor Lavi, who had no escape route."

Thabiti looked at her, his eyebrows wrinkled. "I wasn't actually thinking of Lavi. But why would she need an escape route?"

Chloe pursed her lips. "Surely you've noticed the burns and bruises on her arms and neck. And those are only the ones we can see, as she covers her arms with long sleeved t-shirts, and wears scarves, even in this hot weather."

Thabiti sat up and said in a disbelieving voice, "Oh, I thought she covered herself for religious reasons. But how did she get those injuries? She's not exactly clumsy."

Marina patted his leg and replied, "From her husband. He beats and hurts her."

Thabiti's mouth hung open.

Rose turned to Chloe and said, "I wasn't certain she was a victim of domestic violence, as she kept it well hidden. But I've noticed she barely eats and I doubt she sleeps well. Of course, they are all signals of abuse and it's likely she's felt increasingly isolated."

Chloe moaned, "Oh why didn't she just leave him?"

Marina opened her mouth.

Chloe jumped in, and continued, "I know, Marina, Hindu culture. And of course there don't have to be religious or cultural reasons. I've met women who love their husbands, despite the abuse, but still refuse to leave them. So Lavi's unlikely to have killed Mayur. Anyway, she's such a timid little thing."

Sam looked around the group and said, "Which brings us to jealousy, or resentment…"

"But we haven't finished with hate." Thabiti crossed his arms.

Chloe turned to him, tapping her hand on her thigh. "OK, clever clogs. Who do you think hated Mayur enough to kill him?"

Thabiti leaned forward again and whispered, "Jono!"

The group was silent. Rose felt a fluttering in her tummy. Thabiti might just be right. "Go on," she encouraged.

"I might not be a woman." He looked at Marina.

She dug an elbow into his side.

"Oy!" exclaimed Thabiti. "But I still see things. Like

Lavi and Jono talking together away from everyone else. And Lavi smiling, even giggling, which is the only time she did. I think we've all noticed how grumpy Jono's been in camp, but I don't think he was only worried about the car. I saw the way he glared at Mayur. And it frightened me." Thabiti shuddered.

Rose remembered the conversation from the medical tent and said, "When I visited the medical tent the evening after the crash, I heard Mayur shouting at Lavanya. She ran out in tears and Jono rebuked Mayur, and told him to treat her better. But Mayur retorted that Jono had abandoned Lavanya and she was now his."

Marina drew her eyebrows together. "I know Jono and Lavanya were friends at school."

Chloe gazed intensely round the group and announced, "Jono might have been her boyfriend."

"Shh," said Rose. "Keep your voice down."

Marina met Chloe's eye, "Interesting idea, but I've not heard anyone mention it. But Jono and the Chauhans are hardly popular topics of conversation in our family."

With wide eyes Chloe looked at Sam, then Rose, and asked, "But it is possible that Jono could have suffocated Mayur in the medical tent and then returned to this camp?"

Sam added, "Maybe he did mean to kill Mayur yesterday in the Charge. And he intentionally damaged the winch strop so it would cause an accident."

Marina bobbed in her seat and cried, "And when Mayur was only injured, he finished him off."

Rose mused, "He certainly had the motive and opportunity."

She paused and felt, rather than saw, someone pass them, and then the air was still again.

She heard Chloe plead, "Please don't confront him tonight. He's just found out he didn't kill Vadhana, and after twenty years I think he's allowed one night to savour the news."

Rose murmured, "It may be of little consolation if he killed Mayur."

She looked at the darkness around her. All was quiet, so the camp staff must be in bed, as, she presumed, was Kumar. There were pockets of scattered light beyond the tents from other camps and the central area of headquarters.

She said, "I doubt we'd find him anyway tonight. I thought I heard someone pass a few minutes ago, but I've no idea who it was." She finished the remaining splash of wine in her glass. Sam did the same with his Tusker, tipping his head back and draining the contents of his can.

Marina stood. "I better see what joys await me back at my camp."

Thabiti joined her. "I'll come with you."

"Ladies," said Sam turning to Rose and Chloe as he scrunched his empty can in his huge hands. "Let me walk you back. It's getting late."

CHAPTER FIFTY-FOUR

R ose did not sleep soundly on Tuesday night, as too much information was circulating in her head. Each time she woke, she heard the eerie call of a hyena: a long, low 'oo' sound ending with a high short 'ip'.

At six o'clock, as the darkness thinned, she got up, stuffed her feet into her slippers, and trudged to the loo. There was already activity in the headquarters and she heard the clunking sounds of tents being taken down and the low growl of 4x4 vehicle engines.

Time was running out to discover Mayur's killer before all the competitors, spectators, and officials left, and the headquarters was dismantled until 2017's event.

She stepped out of a Portaloo to be confronted by a fully-dressed and panting Marina.

"I'm so glad I found you. We're packing up. Baba wants to leave before prize-giving, as he wants to avoid the rush." She doubled over and drew breath. "It's Lavi. We can't find her, and her bed hasn't been slept in."

Rose felt a tingling in her numb arthritic fingers and a chill in her bones. All those hyenas she'd heard during the night. She prayed they hadn't found Lavanya. "Let's wake Chloe. She can help us."

As Rose unzipped the tent flap, a groggy Chloe asked, "What time is it?"

"Early," replied Rose. "But Lavanya's missing. So get dressed. We have to find her." Rose tugged jeans, a shirt, and a jumper over her nightie. Chloe put on her bra and top, but pulled a pair of Ugg boots over the bottom of her checked cotton pyjama trousers.

They dashed through headquarters, which was coming to life around them. Marina sprang round a sleepy group of people huddled together cradling hot drinks. Rose and the still-drowsy Chloe followed her at a slower pace.

"I don't like this at all," commented Rose. "A slip of a girl like that out in the Mara on her own."

The bar tent was still standing in readiness for the prize-giving at half past nine. Dormans and the Rusty Nail already had queues of customers. Some stamped their feet against the chilly air whilst others chatted quietly to their neighbours.

Jono stood before them, looking wild. His unruly ginger hair stood up in clumps and his hollow eyes had the look of a frightened antelope.

Thabiti ran to join them. "We've looked all over headquarters, but there's no sign of her."

Chloe rubbed her hands together and asked, "Could she have taken a car and driven home, or somewhere...?"

Jono shook his head. "She can't drive."

"But we'll need to if we're to search for her out in the Mara." Rose looked around. "We need to borrow some cars."

She spotted red-shirted officials in the registration tent. "Wait here."

She dashed into the tent and said quickly, "A woman's gone missing and we need to organise a search party."

Frank Butler looked up. "Rose! Don't worry, she'll soon

reappear. There will be few places to hide once all the tents come down."

"I fear she may have wandered into the Mara."

"Oh dear. But I'm afraid we're all tied up." He threw her a set of keys. "Take my Land Cruiser. It's parked at the entrance."

"Thanks, Frank." She turned to leave, but he called her back.

"Take these as well." He handed her three shortwave radios. "You remember how to use them?"

Rose nodded. She and Craig had often been in charge of a radio at horse shows and the Lewa Marathon.

"I've turned them all to channel 12."

Outside, Jono was frozen with indecision.

She asked him, "Where's Thabiti?"

"Here." Thabiti dashed up, holding up a set of car keys. "Mayur's car."

Rose handed Chloe and Marina radios and gave them a quick lesson on their use.

Then she instructed, "Chloe, you go with Thabiti in Mayur's car. I'll take Jono although I'm not sure how much use he'll be. You turn right out of the gate and begin your search, and we'll turn left."

"What about me?" cried Marina.

Rose took her by the arm and led her away from the group. "I want you to find a pair of binoculars and climb up to your rock, the one we sat on yesterday. There's a great view of the Mara from up there. You're looking for a solitary moving figure or," Rose gulped, "animals gathered together, as that might indicate an injured Lavanya."

Thabiti pulled the silent Jono towards the headquarters' entrance where Rose found Frank's car.

She called to Jono, "Get in."

He meekly complied.

She followed Thabiti, who was driving a large black Land Cruiser Amazon, out of the entrance and they turned away from each other. A pair of black-backed jackals jogged along in front of her along the stony track. She slowly followed them as she surveyed the terrain on either side of the road.

"Jono, snap out of it. I need your help if we're to find Lavanya."

Jono sat up straighter and gazed out of the passenger window.

She followed the road as it veered left out into the grassland, leaving the jackals who continued straight ahead.

She entered a wide plain and spotted a small figure moving along the skyline. Her heart leapt and she left the track and drove towards it. The steering wheel jerked from her grip as she hit a hole.

Steady, she didn't want to damage Frank's car. She slowed down. In the brightening dawn light, she drew closer and watched the graceful figure of a cheetah lope across the wide open space. A wonderful creature, but she had no time to watch it.

She felt a tightness in her chest. How could they hope to find Lavanya out here? It would take days to comprehensively search the area, and by then it would be too late as injured animals did not last long in the Mara. She turned the car eastwards, hoping to pick up another track.

She consoled herself. It was unlikely Lavanya would have wandered too far from headquarters, although nobody knew what time she had left.

CHAPTER FIFTY-FIVE

R ose's radio crackled into life. It was Sam.
"I'm with Marina. And we've found Lavanya."

"Where?" cried Rose.

"Below the rock escarpment. It looks like she's fallen."

That didn't sound good. "She's landed on a ledge, part way down, but she's not moving. Are you driving a silver Land Cruiser?"

"Yes?" Rose hesitated.

"I can see you. Look to your left. Can you make out a rock cliff?"

Rose turned the nose of the car and peered out the windscreen. Half a mile in front of her she saw a darker shape in the landscape. That must be it. "I think so."

"Drive towards it. We might need your help, and the car to move her."

Rose sped forward. "Jono," she nudged him. "They've found her."

"Is she dead?"

"I've no idea, but she will be if we don't help. Come on, get a grip of yourself."

Rose rejoined a track which meandered its way to the foot of the escarpment.

The radio crackled again. "Drive to the far end and look up. You'll see me."

Rose did as instructed. The cliff was lower at this point. Sam stood on the top, but Marina was traversing down the rocks. Her slight figure clung to the rock face like a beetle on a wall.

Rose parked the car and turned to Jono. "Come on. Lavanya needs our help."

Marina stood on a rock ledge, about five metres above Rose.

"She's here." Marina knelt down and cried, "And she's alive."

Rose realised she was shaking and her mouth was dry. She returned to the car and found a bottle of water in a compartment in the driver's side door. Marina was still examining Lavanya.

"It's all my fault," exclaimed Jono.

The noise was so unexpected and painful, like the cry of a wounded animal, that Rose nearly dropped her water bottle. She took a long drink and moved around the front of the car to Jono. This was neither the time nor place for self-pity.

"Drink this." She thrust the water bottle into his hand.

He took a long slug and then called to Marina. "How is she?"

Marina had removed her jacket and Rose presumed she'd draped it over Lavanya. "She's cold and I don't like the look of her leg. Rose, can you climb up here? And do you have a medical kit?"

Rose looked at the cliff and flexed her arthritic fingers. There was another ledge below Marina which ran down to the edge of the cliff. At that point it was less than a metre above ground level. "I might be able to get to you with Jono's help. Let me check what kit is in the car."

The boot of the car held more small bottles of water, a shuka blanket and a first aid kit stuffed inside a net in the rear door. She grabbed two bottles of water, the other equipment and returned to Jono.

"I'm guessing you were a rugby player, perhaps even a cricketer. I need you to throw these up to Marina."

Jono threw a bottle of water, but it bounced back down the cliff face. She collected the dented bottle and said encouragingly, "Come on, concentrate. You can do this. For Lavanya."

Jono took aim and Marina caught the bottle. Re-energised, he threw the second water bottle and the first aid kit.

Rose asked, "Can you bring the blanket? And I'll need your help getting onto that ledge."

They strode to the end of the cliff. Jono held his cupped hand for her to step in. She grabbed hold of the ledge and with Jono's upward thrust scrambled onto it. "Thanks. Can you hand me the blanket?"

Slowly and carefully she edged along the narrow shelf of rock. Every so often, she shook her hands. It was so frustrating that they refused to grip the rock, but she tried her best to encourage blood to flow through them. She grasped a larger chunk of rock, but it came away in her hand and she balanced precariously on the edge.

"Careful," shouted Jono below her. She grabbed at a protruding tree root, held on and pulled herself back to the rock face. Her heart pounded against it. At last Jono seemed galvanised. She looked down and saw him shadowing her journey. He waited with open arms in case she fell, which only felt partially reassuring. It looked a long way down.

Finally she arrived under Marina's ledge. "Here, take

this." She passed up the blanket. Marina took her hand and hauled her up onto the ledge. The scrapes on her legs stung, even through her trousers.

She knelt down on the solid rock and gently shook Lavanya's inert form. "Lavanya, are you awake? Can you hear me?"

Lavanya groaned.

"Has she had any water?" She looked up at Marina.

"Not yet."

She splashed water onto Lavanya's dry lips. The girl licked them and tried to sit up.

"Careful." She was worried about damaging Lavanya's neck. "Try not to move just yet. Can you feel your toes?"

"Not sure," Lavanya's faint voice answered. 'I'm so cold."

Rose shuffled along the ledge and lifted the blanket. Lavanya wore a single flip flop. Her feet would be numb from the night chill. Marina was correct though, the lower part of her left leg was at an awkward angle beneath her right one. She touched it.

"Ow," cried Lavanya.

Rose stroked her arm and said, "Please be brave. I just need to take a look at your leg."

Marina knelt down and took hold of Lavanya's hand as Rose rolled up her trouser leg. There was a gash, a lot of dried blood, and some nasty looking purple bruises. "Broken leg," she mouthed to Marina.

Rose looked up but could not see Sam. "Sam, are you still there?"

"Yes, I am. How are you doing?"

"We're going to need some help. Her leg is broken but we can't leave her here. We're going to have to find a way to move her off this ledge."

Sam shouted back. "I can run back to headquarters and

find a backboard, and some helpers, but I'll need a car. Jono can you drive back and pick me up?"

Jono shook his head. "I don't drive."

"Don't or can't?" yelled Sam.

"Not since the accident. Since I crashed my car and killed Vadhana."

"But you didn't crash your car," Rose called. "You weren't driving. You said just now that it's your fault Lavanya is lying here. So you need to make it right. You have to drive the car back to headquarters and fetch help. She can't stay out here all day. Not with the rising temperature, and we won't be able to fend off lions or hyenas once they smell dried blood."

Jono still hesitated.

"Please," pleaded Marina.

As if in a trance, Jono moved to the driver's door. He opened it and peered inside.

Rose called down, "The keys are still in the ignition. It's an automatic."

Jono heaved himself into the driver's seat and turned the key. For a moment he sat there with the engine idling. Then he closed the door and drove forward, erratically at first, before he turned onto the track and sped away.

"I'm going for help," shouted Sam. "Will you two be OK?"

"Yes," Rose and Marina called back in unison.

CHAPTER FIFTY-SIX

Thabiti and Chloe met Sam when they returned to headquarters. Chloe jumped out of the car before Thabiti had turned off the ignition, and rushed across to Sam.

Thabiti extracted himself and heard Chloe exclaim, "We received your message and got back as quickly as we could. Where's Lavi?"

Sam placed a large hand on her shoulder and said, "Steady. She's lying on a rock shelf near the bottom of a cliff. Marina and Mama Rose are with her, and Jono is driving back here to collect me."

Chloe started. "But Jono told me he doesn't drive."

"Mama Rose persuaded him. I had no idea how long you'd be getting back and we have to move Lavanya off that ledge."

Thabiti joined them. "How will you get her down? Is she injured?"

Sam rubbed his arm. "Mama Rose thinks she has a broken leg, but it was a long fall, so there may be other injuries. She certainly can't get down herself, even with assistance, so we'll have to get her down."

"What do you suggest?" asked Thabiti.

"That we use a backboard. Marina and Mama Rose could roll her onto it, strap her in, and pass her down to me."

Chloe frowned. 'What if she slips off? How far down is it?"

"I'm not sure," conceded Sam.

Thabiti thought for a moment and then suggested, "How about you lower the backboard down on ropes, strap her on, and lower her to the bottom."

"Great idea," cried Chloe. "Are you strong enough to help Sam? It's a job for two people."

"I'll do it." Jono strode towards them. His skin was pallid and his eyes sunken but alert. His jaw was set. "I'll fetch some ropes from the car, whilst you find a backboard."

They regrouped ten minutes later. Jono carried two nylon ropes.

"The medics have left," panted Chloe. "But Wendy helped us and we found a backboard at the rear of the registration tent. Wendy called Amref but it'll be four hours before they can get a plane here."

"I'll fly her to Nairobi." Jono clenched his fists. "We'll need a car to collect her and drive her to the airstrip. Thabiti, can you and Chloe drive to the bottom of the cliff?" He gave them directions.

"Ready Sam?" he asked.

Sam picked up the backboard and strode towards the cliff. Jono followed with the ropes.

CHAPTER FIFTY-SEVEN

R ose saw that Marina was shivering. The sun was hidden by the cliff face and had not begun to warm their ledge.

She said, "Why don't you put your jacket back on? Lavanya has the shuka helping to warm her up now, and I don't need two patients to deal with."

Marina stood, flapped her arms, and began to bounce up and down on the soles of her feet as if she was doing a weird on-the-spot run. "If I keep moving, it will help keep me warm. Lavi needs the jacket more than me, as she can't get up and move around."

"Ok, if you're sure." Rose opened the first aid kit and searched about until she found both paracetamol and ibuprofen. She chose the ibuprofen as it would help reduce any inflammation, as well as pain for Lavanya.

She reached for the water and spoke gently to Lavanya, "I've found some painkillers. Would you like one?"

Lavanya nodded.

Marina knelt down and helped support Lavanya as she swallowed the painkiller with some water, and laid her carefully back on the rock, pulling the blanket up.

Rose flexed her fingers which still ached and pulled at her yellow official's bracelet which rubbed against her wrist. A thought tugged at her. She pulled down the blanket and lifted each of Lavanya's arms. Although each had a series of bruises or burns there was no bracelet.

"It's shocking isn't it. Even more so that she managed to keep it hidden from everyone," commented Marina. "But that's not what concerns you at the moment is it?"

"I was wondering where her Rhino Charge bracelet is, as she's not wearing one. What colour would it be?"

Marina pulled back her own sleeve. "Blue like mine. I was a supporter and didn't bother to change it when I joined the Bandit Bush Hog team. But why does it matter? We're leaving today."

Rose thought back to the previous morning. It was only yesterday that she'd discovered Mayur's body. She remembered the pools of water on the floor and the blanket. But there was something else, a blue piece of plastic partially hidden by the blanket. It had holes in the end just like a Rhino Charge bracelet, a blue supporter's one.

Lavanya stirred. "I'm thirsty. Can I have more water?" She shuffled and lifted her head to sip from the bottle. "Thank you. I'm so sorry to cause all this trouble."

"Don't you worry. Just rest." Rose's voice was soothing.

But Marina's was tense as she asked, "Why did you run away?"

"I didn't, not really. I heard you talking last night, and you were discussing Jono and me. You said you thought he killed Mayur... because of me." Tears slipped down Lavanya's cheeks and splashed onto the grey rock.

"Well it makes sense." Marina sat down and stretched her legs out along the rock behind Lavanya.

"I swear he didn't do it. I love him so much." She sniffed. "But Mayur knew, and he taunted me. After a while I just ignored him, until he gleefully announced Jono was back. He kept saying Jono no longer cared for me, because he hadn't called or visited me."

Rose smoothed hair away from Lavanya's forehead. The poor girl was so torn up inside. "It's OK," she murmured.

Lavanya shook her head. "No, it's not. Mayur persuaded Kumar to ask Jono to join the Rhino Charge team just to torment me. But I was so excited that I would see Jono again. But in camp, Jono was so miserable and kept complaining about Deepak Seth. He said he'd never be free."

Lavanya tried to sit up, but Marina caught her head and rested it on her thigh. "I didn't know what to do when I heard about the accident. I thought something awful had happened to Jono. But then officials spoke with Kumar and explained Mayur had been badly injured, but there was no Amref plane to collect him and airlift him to a hospital in Nairobi."

Rose rubbed her hands together. A shaft of sunlight lit the rock as the sun climbed higher in the sky. Lavanya tried to sit up again, but Rose took her head and laid it back on Marina's thigh and said, "Steady, you must be careful,"

Lavanya tried to jerk her head up again, as she said, "But I need to tell you. Nobody ever listens to me."

Rose stroked her cheek. "It's OK. We're not going anywhere and we're listening. Go on."

Lavanya relaxed and continued. "I helped Kumar across to the medical tent, but I was shocked to find both Mayur and Jono inside. Mayur was furious, not about his injuries, but about the accident costing him the Rhino Charge title. Kumar and Jono told him he'd had a lucky escape. But he ranted on, first about Thabiti for his failings as a mechanic, then at Kumar for having such a sub-standard team, and finally at Jono and me."

Rose realised Lavanya hadn't been able to talk to anyone. They'd all been so busy rushing around proving Thabiti's innocence and getting to the bottom of the crash. Lavanya had hovered on the edge, but none of them had stopped to see how she was. And to really take an interest in her.

They had seen the bruises and burns, but ignored them, believing it wasn't their place. Rose chastised herself. If only she'd taken the time to sit down with Lavanya. Maybe she could have prevented the tragedy.

The words spilled out of Lavanya. "I was so scared. Mayur's eyes flashed. He was manic and boasted that I was his, and that Jono and I would never be together. He said he would treat me any way he wanted and there was nothing Jono could do about it."

Her tears cascaded onto the rock. "Kumar was furious with Mayur. He told him to be grateful as I'd cost him a high bride price and I should be treated with respect. But that only incensed Jono, who chastised Kumar, telling him it was inhumane to buy a bride. It wasn't surprising that Kumar wanted to leave, and of course I had to help him."

Rose placed a hand on Lavanya's shoulder and asked, "But you returned?"

Lavanya nodded. "Yes. I didn't want Jono to blame Kumar. He's helped my family so much, and has given my father and brother jobs, and a bride price is a Hindu tradition. But Mayur wouldn't let me speak to Jono and shouted horrible things at me in Hindi. And he twisted and hurt my wrist. So Jono started shouting at Mayur and I was worried about what he would do to him. It was all too much, so I ran away."

Lavanya sobbed. "I tried to please Mayur, to make it up to him. I took him some food, but because I also gave some to Jono, he shouted and threatened us both."

"Jono must have been furious," remarked Marina. "No wonder he smothered Mayur. I would have done the same just to shut him up."

CHAPTER FIFTY-EIGHT

S am shouted from the top of the cliff. "Are you all right
down there?"

"Yes," called Rose.

"Thabiti and Chloe will be there in a minute. They're
driving round to you. Jono's with me and we're going to
lower a backboard down to you. Can you strap Lavanya onto
it? Then we'll work out how to manoeuvre her to the
ground."

"OK," Rose yelled.

Several minutes later, she heard a clatter and Sam
shouted, "Nearly there. We'll have to swing it over that rock
which juts out above you. Watch your heads."

An orange board swung out and down towards them.
Marina grabbed hold of it and handed it to Rose, as she gently
removed Lavanya's head from her thigh and stood up. She
took the board back and yelled, "I've got it. Can you lower it
a bit more?" Marina guided the board onto a space between
the cliff face and Lavanya.

Rose knelt behind Lavanya's head and explained to
Marina. "I'm going to roll her carefully away from the board.

Can you slip it underneath her? Be brave, my dear," she said to Lavanya. "We'll have you down soon, but this may hurt."

Lavanya cried out as Rose rolled her away from and then back onto the board.

"We just need to shuffle you on a bit more, and strap you in securely."

"Ow!" moaned Lavanya

"Nearly there." Rose sat up and looked at Marina, "OK?"

Marina nodded.

"Tighten the straps carefully, but they must be secure so she doesn't move."

A black Land Cruiser Amazon purred to a stop below them and Thabiti and Chloe stepped out. Chloe shaded her eyes and called, "Is everything OK?"

"Yes, we're nearly there," responded Rose, returning to her patient.

"Ready," Marina shouted to Sam.

Sam shouted back instructions. "Hold onto each end of the board. Push it to the edge of the ledge. Have you done that?"

"Yes."

"Hold the board whilst we pull up the slack." The two ropes at either end of the board became taught. "Now push the board out."

Chloe cried out as the board plummeted several feet before jolting to a halt.

"Don't drop me," screamed Lavanya.

Rose heard Jono's voice. "Don't worry, we've got you." Rose peered over the edge, watching Lavanya's descent until Chloe and Thabiti took hold of the board and guided it to the ground.

"What about you two?" called Thabiti.

Marina stood. She collected the empty water bottles and

first aid kit. "Catch these," she shouted at Thabiti and threw the items, one by one.

"She turned to Rose. "If I go first. I can help you lower yourself onto the ledge you used to get up here. Is that OK?"

Rose looked about and said, "It'll have to be. I'm not sitting up here all day as live animal bait." She looked down.

"It's not far," shouted Chloe.

It was all right for her to say. It looked a long way from where Rose sat. She turned away from the edge and gingerly lowered herself. Marina took some of her weight and steered her onto the narrow stone ledge. Rose's arms stung. She had scraped them on the way down.

"Don't look down," instructed Marina. "Watch the rock face in front of you and shuffle your way along. Tell me if you want to stop." It was a slow, tiring journey and Rose was relieved when Marina helped her onto terra firma. As her legs began to buckle beneath her, Thabiti rushed forward and supported her.

"Thank you."

Sam shouted from the top of the cliff. "Is everyone OK?"

Rose looked up and saw him standing next to Jono.

"We're good," shouted Marina.

"Can you untie the ropes? We'll reel them back up."

Marina and Chloe undid the ropes. Rose, able to support her weight again, joined them and bent over Lavanya. She asked, "Are you all right? That was quite an ordeal."

"Jono," muttered Lavanya. "Where's Jono?"

"He's at the top of the cliff. He helped rescue you, and get you down from the ledge where you'd fallen."

Lavanya grasped Rose's sleeve. "I didn't jump. I thought about it, but I didn't. It was dark and I must have tripped."

"There, there, it's OK." Rose covered Lavanya's hand.

"Can I tell you a secret?" Lavanya whispered.

Jono shouted, "We're done. Meet you at the airstrip."

"Watch out," called Thabiti to Rose.

He manoeuvred the backboard, with Marina and Chloe's help, into the car boot and slid it along and up onto the top of a lowered rear seat.

Rose opened a back door and locked eyes with Lavanya. "Are you comfortable?"

Lavanya gripped her shirt with surprising strength, pulled her forwards and whispered, "Jono didn't kill Mayur. I did."

She gently removed Lavanya's hand and replied, "I know, dear."

CHAPTER FIFTY-NINE

Thabiti drove with surprising care to the airstrip, but the car still jolted over bumps and holes in the track and each time it did, Lavanya groaned.

Chloe was sitting next to Lavanya's head, and she pleaded, "Please be brave. We have to get you to Jono and the airplane so he can fly you to hospital in Nairobi."

They arrived at the Mara airstrip and found Sam waiting for them, whilst Jono was busy with pre-flight safety checks.

Rose approached Jono "Are you ready? Do you want Thabiti to come with you?"

"I'm fine." He watched Lavanya being lifted out of the car and transferred across to the plane. "Actually, it might be best if Thabiti does come along. Just in case Lavi needs anything."

Rose lowered her voice and asked, "When did you realise she killed Mayur?" She followed him as he moved down the side of the plane.

He didn't look at her, but answered, "She was in a state the morning after the accident, but at first I wasn't surprised. Mayur had been beastly to her the previous evening, but even so, I began to think something else was bothering her.

She had bruising around her wrist from where Mayur had grabbed her and twisted it. But when I looked closely at it I noticed more scarring on her arm. I asked her about it, but she clammed up. She's been alone for so long with nobody to talk to that I suppose she couldn't bring herself to confide in anyone about the abuse she's suffered, not even me."

Jono opened a panel in the side of the plane. Rose kept quiet whilst he checked various dials. She felt the plane rock as Lavanya was lifted in. She wondered how they would secure her. Sam would organise that. She needed to get to the bottom of Mayur's death.

Jono closed the panel, but continued to stare at it. "Later I realised she was missing her security bracelet. I returned to the medical tent to check, but you were there and the tent had been cleared. If I hadn't been worrying about Deepak, the old accident, and the new one, I might have realised sooner how she was feeling, and stopped her before she took such drastic action."

Jono turned to Rose. "I don't know how she did it. She doesn't look strong enough, but I guess she was so desperate, so terrorised that she saw no other way out. If only she had come to me, I could have helped. Mayur didn't scare me. If only she'd waited, as now I'm free of the shackles of twenty years of guilt, I can begin a new life. We could have. Together. Despite Mayur's bravado and their Hindu culture I would have taken her away from him. And now?"

He held his hands up. "I've gone from one nightmare straight into another. I doubt I'll ever be free of guilt or be truly happy."

Sam appeared. "We're ready."

Jono sniffed. "Two minutes," he called back.

Rose left Jono and strode around to the other side of the plane. She saw that Lavanya had been strapped to the floor and she looked drowsy, which was probably the shock of her ordeal taking over. Hopefully she'd sleep on the journey.

Rose didn't disturb her but approached Thabiti and asked, "Can you go with Jono? He may need your help in Nairobi. And some support after all he's been through."

"I'll be his wing man." Thabiti beamed and handed Mayur's car keys to Sam.

Jono sat in the pilot seat, put on his headphones, and checked more dials. Sam pulled Rose and Chloe out of the way and they joined Marina by the car. Thabiti waved and climbed aboard.

Jono removed his headphones and shouted out of the small window. "Don't worry, I'll be back to pick you up."

"Wow," said Chloe. She looked down at her dusty Ugg boots and checked pyjama trousers. "I think I should change, and then, as Thabiti isn't here to say it, breakfast anyone?"

CHAPTER SIXTY

At nine o'clock the catering area was busy with competitors eating breakfast before the prize-giving. They proudly wore their rainbow of coloured team tops. Sam was seated at a table away from the main group and Marina was with him, a holdall on the floor beside her. They were both eating breakfast rolls. Sam pushed wrapped breakfast rolls towards Rose and Chloe and two large paper cups.

"Thanks, Sam," exclaimed Chloe. "Fantastic, a Dormans cappuccino."

"And a Kericho Gold Tea." Rose was grateful for the warm sweet tea and the roll which she bit into without really tasting. What a morning. She felt light-headed, whether from the mornings events or the lack of food, she was unsure.

Marina announced, "My family have left me. All that was left in camp was my bag. What a caring bunch they are."

Rose placed an arm round her shoulder. "Don't worry, we'll organise a lift for you."

Sam put his roll down. "I visited Kumar and told him we'd found Lavanya. I said she was injured, so Jono was flying her to Nairobi."

Rose cradled her cup. "Oh, well done. I need to see him again, and explain what's happened. But first I need five minutes' peace." She sipped her tea and allowed her thoughts to drift. She was aware of Marina and Chloe quizzing Sam about his role in the anti-poaching unit and receiving guarded responses.

The play *Romeo and Juliet* came to mind. Feuding families and desperate lovers. Juliet sacrificing herself for the love of Romeo. Rose felt that in the heat of the moment, either Lavanya or Jono could have killed Mayur, but Jono was able to pull himself back from the edge, maybe because he'd already lived so long with the guilt of causing someone's death.

Lavanya. Quiet, timid, Lavanya. Cooking, waiting on tables, helping her elderly, injured father-in-law whilst being subjected to physical, verbal and emotional abuse from a bullying husband. Rose couldn't comprehend the effect of this or how Lavanya could have remained in such a frightening relationship. But she'd helped friends leave violent husbands and several had struggled, even after many years, with the feelings of guilt and inadequacy.

She had to tell Kumar that his daughter-in-law had killed his son. Would he be entirely surprised? Would he feel any remorse? Could he have averted the tragic event? But that was for his own conscience.

Lavanya had taken a life which broke the common law and the law of God, whether you followed the Hindu or the Catholic religion. But still, did Lavanya deserve to die as well, or should she swap the confinement of her marriage for that of imprisonment? It would be up to the Kenya legal system and courts now.

"I'm ready to see Kumar."

Sam, Marina, and Chloe looked at her expectantly. Chloe asked, "So are you going to tell us who killed Mayur?"

"Not until after I've spoken with Kumar. Marina, can you come with me? Chloe, why don't you stay with Sam and enjoy the prize-giving? When it's finished, join us at the Bandit Bush Hog's camp."

CHAPTER SIXTY-ONE

R ose entered the partially dismantled Bandit Bush Hog camp. Marina accompanied her, bent under the weight of the holdall she carried over her shoulder. Kumar sat alone in the events shelter with white plastic chairs stacked behind him. The spotted PVC tablecloth had been removed, leaving a marked wooden trestle table.

Kumar looked old, and his skin was lined and blotchy. "They've all gone. They've left me."

"Jono and Thabiti will be back soon. I think Sam told you that Lavanya fell off an escarpment and was injured, so she's been flown to Nairobi for immediate treatment."

"But what shall I do? How can I get home?"

Marina stepped forward and patted Kumar on the shoulder. "I'll help. I can drive us both back to Nairobi."

He looked up at her. "That's kind of you. You were in the team, weren't you, with my son? He's dead now, you know."

Marina looked across at Rose with raised eyebrows.

Rose wondered how she was going to break the news of Lavanya's betrayal to Kumar when he was in this state. But she had to try. She sat down next to Kumar and laid a hand on his arm. "I know who killed Mayur."

"My son," he cried. "My oldest son." He turned to Rose. "I failed him, you know."

"In what way?" asked Rose, surprised by Kumar's reaction.

"I should have been stronger. I should have stood up to him. I should have stood up to his mother." Kumar turned away from Rose and kneaded his forehead.

Rose waited patiently.

Kumar took a deep breath, turned back to Rose and held her gaze. "Mayur was always a difficult child and so full of anger. If he was playing a board game and losing, he'd throw everything on the floor, and if something didn't work, or he was frustrated, he'd throw it at me or his mother. But rather than chastising him, she always forgave him. She'd hug him and tell him it didn't matter and give him a biscuit or piece of cake."

Kumar tapped his fingers on the table. "He got worse when his brother was born, probably because his mother's attention was diverted away from him. One day I saw him playing with his toy cars and when he thought I wasn't watching, he hit his baby brother on the head with a metal truck. And it continued into school, where he was always getting into trouble. I would try and punish him and he'd always run to his mother who told him not to worry and to ignore my punishment. What could I do when I was constantly undermined?"

Rose didn't know what to say, so she felt that it was better to just listen.

"I thought he had grown out of it at secondary school, as he didn't get into trouble nearly as much, and he did really well on the sports field, particularly rugby. But he only became more devious and better at concealing his actions. I found this out when one of my workers brought his daughter to me. She had refused Mayur's advances, so he'd sexually and physically assaulted her. I snapped and banished him to work in the UK. I guess I thought that out of sight was out of mind."

Kumar shook his head. "But he still contacted his mother, begging to be allowed home. She eventually persuaded me that if he found a steady, calm, but intelligent, girl, Mayur would settle down. She said he wanted to start a family and join the business. It was she who suggested Lavanya as a potential wife. Now I think about it, I bet the two of them hatched the plan together. Mayur probably only wanted Lavanya because she had been unobtainable at school, and he knew she loved Jono."

Rose sat up in surprise.

Kumar leaned towards her and said, "Oh, I know all about Jono now. Lavanya told me about him last night. And about Mayur tormenting her and telling her she loved a killer, a criminal, and that she'd never see him again. But when Jono returned to Kenya, apparently Mayur was even worse. I only asked Jono to join the team at Mayur's suggestion. For once I thought he was being thoughtful and involving an old friend. How wrong could I have been?"

Rose crossed her hands in her lap. "And did you know about the abuse? That Mayur hit and burnt your daughter-in-law?"

Tears welled in Kumar's eyes. "Not at first. I denied it. I knew he shouted at her and made her cry. When I saw the marks, I just thought she was clumsy. But my younger son confronted me a few weeks ago. And he told me he couldn't stand by as Mayur's violence against Lavanya escalated. He said he would report Mayur to the police unless I did something about it. So I asked him to give me time to think about it, and I have been doing so this weekend. I'd decided to return Lavanya to her parents, or if not there, any place she wanted to go to. Somewhere she would feel safe."

Kumar ran the back of his hand across his eyes and sniffed. "I told her this last night and she broke down. She said she'd been thinking of running away, but wasn't sure where to go. She wanted to help people, and be somewhere Mayur wouldn't find her. Apparently she'd applied to join a congregation of Catholic sisters, who she said used love and compassion to bring medical care, education, and relief from poverty in remote areas in Kenya."

Rose said, "I know the Congregation of the Sisters of Mercy. They do excellent work here and internationally."

Kumar laid his hand on the table, "But Lavanya is a Hindu. Why would she want to give up her faith?"

Rose placed her hand over Kumar's. "Perhaps she didn't see it as giving up her faith, but as an opportunity to help people. I'm sure there are Hindu organisations in India who do similar work, but how would Lavanya get there?"

Marina stood beside Rose and uncharacteristically asked, "Can I speak?"

Kumar looked up at her in surprise. "Of course, my dear."

Marina twisted her fingers. "It's just that we were discussing religion around the campfire a few nights ago. I mentioned my own struggles with the Hindu faith, in that it tends to segregate people by the caste into which they are born. And that I find it hard to comprehend that a person's actions do not affect this life but the next."

" Lavanya didn't say much, but I think she agreed. She will always be considered beneath us for being from the Shudra caste. And it was because of this that she had to give up her medical training and her dreams of becoming a doctor. She was told to marry Mayur." Marina kept her eyes on the ground.

Kumar placed a hand on her arm. "You young people see things differently, so perhaps you are right. Perhaps she sees her calling as helping people and she cannot do it within the confines of her current religion."

Rose leant back and said, "Unfortunately, she won't be able to help many people from the confines of a prison cell. Did she tell you last night that she killed Mayur?"

Kumar looked directly at Rose and said simply, "Yes."

"So will you go to the police or wait for them to approach you? They may be on their way now."

"Yes, yes, of course. But what do I tell them? That my son beat his wife and I stood by and did nothing until he pushed her to the point where she killed him? And of course they will expect me to pay."

Marina gasped, "But surely they won't charge you as well. You didn't kill your son."

Kumar grunted, "But I didn't stop it, either. But that's not what I meant. The Kenyan authorities will expect me to pay to prosecute my daughter-in-law for murdering my son."

Marina exclaimed, "But you can't do that, can you?"

Kumar looked up, "I need justice for my son. And besides, if I don't pay there will be no trial and Lavanya will be left to rot in prison without any hope of being released. The process takes long enough as it is."

Marina extracted a plastic chair from the pile behind Kumar and sat down opposite Rose. She asked, "What's it like in prison?"

Rose answered, "Cold and bare. My only experience is visiting the women in Nanyuki prison. Their accommodation is overcrowded and they have to fight for a space sharing a mattress, otherwise there is only the concrete floor. And there isn't enough food to go round. Prisoners can buy extra rations, but for that they need someone to visit regularly and leave money at the shop."

Marina shivered despite the warmth of the sun. "I can't

see Lavanya fighting for her corner. More likely she'd just curl up in one and wither away."

Rose leant across and laid a hand on Marina's arm. "I know, it's not very pleasant, and I agree with you that Lavanya might not survive, but she does have considerable inner strength. After all, she put up with Mayur's verbal, emotional, and physical abuse for many years."

Marina jumped up and her chair fell back. "But Mr Chauhan, surely you won't pay to send Lavanya to jail and almost certain death?"

Kumar wiped tears from his eyes. "But my dear, what else can I do? It is the law."

Marina righted her chair and Rose said in a small, calm voice, "Of course, the police don't know Lavanya killed Mayur. We and Lavanya are the only ones who know that."

Marina turned round and leant against the table which wobbled. "Yes, that's right. Please Mr Chauhan. There has to be another way. I know you want justice for your son, but what about Lavanya? Doesn't she deserve some justice and some understanding after all she's suffered? Please don't give her up to the police."

Kumar leaned back and looked up at the cobalt-blue sky. "I don't disagree with you. I know Lavanya acted out of a combination of desperation and self-defence, seeing only pain and suffering ahead of her, in her marriage and her life. But what alternative is there?"

Rose rubbed her chin and said, "Well you once punished your son with banishment. Is it something you would consider for Lavanya? She mentioned joining the Catholic mission. I might be able to help find her a place there. I don't think she would have to become a nun, not at first anyway, but she would be safe and helping some of our poorest communities."

Sam and Nick West strode into camp between the leleshwa bushes, accompanied by two overweight policemen.

"Good morning, Kumar," said Nick. "These gentlemen would like to speak to you about the death of your son."

Rose stood and offered her chair to the senior officer.

He sat down, looked up at Rose and sneered, "And I'll have a coffee and a steak sandwich with chips, please."

The other police officer, who had taken Marina's vacant seat, said, "And I'll have the same."

Kumar's shoulders slumped as he pulled three thousand bob notes from his pocket. He handed them to Marina and said in a monotone voice, "Would you mind fetching the officers' order?" He turned to the policemen and asked, "So who killed my son?"

CHAPTER SIXTY-TWO

Nick, Rose, and Sam walked through the leleshwa
bushes out of the Bandit Bush Hog's camp.

Nick turned to Rose and said, "I'm sorry you couldn't
find out who killed Mayur, but now the police are here,
perhaps it's better to leave the matter with them. Thank you
for all your help."

He held his hand out to Sam, who shook it. "And thank
you for helping Rose. Can I leave you to liaise with the Narok
police? Let me know if you need anything or if they want to
speak to me again, although I'm not sure what I can add."

Nick left them as Marina returned with a paper bag
hanging from her arm.

She carried a cup in each hand. "Please, take these," she
beseeched Sam.

Sam grabbed the cups and Marina let the bag slide to the
floor.

She shook her arms. "Ow, those were hot and the bag was
getting heavy."

Sam balanced one coffee cup on top of the other and bent
down for the bag. "I'll take these to the policemen and check
if Kumar needs any help."

Marina peered after Sam through the gap in the leleshwa bushes. "What do you think Mr Chauhan is telling those awful policemen?"

"Shh," chided Rose.

"I don't know how you can be so calm. They were really rude to you," Marina whispered, but her voice was still loud.

"It's best to just ignore people like that... but I hope I don't have to be interviewed by them."

Sam pushed his way back through the leleshwa bushes and said, "I think they're nearly finished. I hope Kumar's all right, as he's very red in the face. I'd say he's rather angry."

Marina did whisper this time, "But what has he told them?"

"I gather very little," replied Sam. "But then what can he tell them? He's spent most of his time in his camp. I heard him say he didn't know anyone who would want to kill his son."

Rose looked at Marina who was completely still and staring at Sam with her mouth open. Rose breathed deeply and relaxed. Surely this meant Kumar had decided banishment was a better punishment than a Nairobi jail.

And if these policemen were anything to go by, she doubted he would want them, or anyone else, sneering at him as they washed his family's dirty laundry in public.

Sam looked at Rose and then Marina. "Have I missed something?" he asked.

"That's what I want to know." Chloe jogged up to them. She stopped and placed her hands on her hips, panting slightly.

"Hi, Chloe. What have you been up to?"

Chloe caught her breath. "I've been packing up our things. Wendy Butler caught me and said the hire company wanted to take down the officials' tents. I've left everything in a pile by the entrance to the official's camp so I hope it'll be all right."

Chloe stepped back from the gap in the leleshwa bushes as the two policemen emerged. They ignored the women and spoke solely to Sam. "There was little the victim's father could tell us, and he wasn't particularly cooperative. We'll keep the case open, but I'm not sure there's much else we can do, not now that potential witnesses are leaving the scene. Is there anyone else we should speak to?"

Sam looked over the shoulders of the policemen at Rose, but she gave a barely perceptible shake of the head.

"Not that I can think of," replied Sam. "Would you like me to walk you to your car?"

"No thank you. We can make our own way. We better head back to Narok and stop by the check point we set up on the Mara to Narok road this morning." He looked around and smiled. "A profitable venture, I should think."

They strode away.

Marina's face was contorted. "Profitable venture indeed. Taking bribes from everyone leaving the Charge more like it. I doubt they're interested in any hard work, like finding Mayur's killer. They only want to take advantage, and make a quick profit from people who have long journeys and don't want to be delayed with police bureaucracy. Mind you, I'll have to be very careful driving back."

Rose looked across at Sam who was staring at her.

He asked, "Well?"

She responded quickly. "Let's go and check on Kumar."

Kumar was still sitting at the table, although the events shelter had been dismantled and two of the camp staff were trying to force its covering into a travelling bag.

He turned round as Rose, Sam, Chloe, and Marina approached him. "It's done," he called. "I couldn't throw

Lavanya to those wolves of policemen. They had no interest in truth or justice. And they would have tried to bleed every shilling they could from me. I will visit Lavanya when she has recovered and discuss our proposition. Could you see if there is a vacancy at one of the Sisters of Mercy's missions?"

Rose stepped forward and cupped Kumar's hands in her own. "You are both brave and compassionate. May whichever god is looking down on us bless you."

Sam stepped forward. "I think I have an inkling of what happened, and it was better I didn't know before I spoke to those policemen, but it's clear you knew, Mama Rose, and you didn't want to be interviewed by them."

Kumar looked up at Sam. "This is to go no further."

Chloe and Marina edged forward.

"Lavanya killed my son. His abuse of her, both emotional and physical, was too much. I think the catalyst this weekend was Jono, her old flame. She snapped and somehow suffocated Mayur." He bowed his head and rubbed his temples. "Such a waste. Two lives ruined."

Marina asked nervously, "But Mr Chauhan. Mayur was large and strong and Lavanya, well, she's so timid and petite. How could she have done it?"

Rose replied, "I don't think we shall ever know. I can only guess that she crept back to the medical tent when Mayur was asleep and caught him off-guard. She may have used a pillow and Mayur was partially incapacitated with an injured arm. I guess she clung to him like a lioness which has jumped on the back of a large buffalo."

Kumar held up his hands. "And that, everyone, is the end of it. I would appreciate it if you did not discuss this further, even amongst yourselves. Please respect my wishes on this matter."

Rose, Sam, Chloe, and Marina each murmured their ascent.

Marina collected her bag from beside the pile of chairs. "Well, If you're ready, Mr Chauhan, I would like to get going. We have a long drive back to Nairobi."

Rose announced, "So this is the end of the 2016 Rhino Charge."

CHAPTER SIXTY-THREE

On Friday morning, Rose and Chloe once again flew over the Aberdare Mountain range, and their pilot was Jono Urquhart. He was flying tourists down to Wilson Airport so Rose and Chloe were squashed together at the back. They exited the mountains smoothly and flew on over the Great Rift Valley and its escarpment before landing at Wilson Airport.

They waited patiently by the plane while Jono escorted the tourists through the single storey departure building.

Jono opened the door of a black Land Cruiser Amazon. "Ready, ladies?"

"Are you driving?" enquired Chloe. "Whose car is it?"

Jono's eyebrows drew together. "You might think it ironic, but Kumar gave me Mayur's car. So now I've no excuse not to drive. If it's OK, I'll drive us back to Nanyuki in it this afternoon."

Jono turned left onto the slow-moving Langata Road and the source of the queue was soon apparent.

"Is that allowed?" exclaimed Chloe.

Ahead of them two Maasai herdsmen casually shepherded

their cows down the centre of the road, seemingly oblivious to the oncoming traffic.

Rose chuckled. "Believe it or not, they have the right of way."

It took them a further twenty minutes to travel the relatively short distance to the Karen Hospital where they found Lavanya in a private room on the second floor. She was reading the Bible.

Jono scowled and said in a disdainful tone, "So you're really going ahead with this mad scheme?"

Lavanya held his gaze. Her skin was pallid, but her cheeks had filled out. "What choice do I have? Kumar has been very generous, and I don't want to rot away in prison. Besides, now I can help people, which is what I've always wanted to do. And perhaps my experience will be useful in helping other women in similar situations."

Jono pleaded, "But what about us?"

She placed the Bible, open but upside down, on the white sheet. "It was just not meant to be. We are destined to tread different paths. This is mine, and you now need to discover what yours is."

Lavanya turned to Rose. "Thank you for everything, and this opportunity of starting a new life. Do you know, I feel a calling, and a strong desire to do this?"

Chloe stepped forward and asked, "How is Kumar?"

"He visits me most days, but he seems much older. He told me he's handing the company over to his younger son, who is going to begin discussions with the Seths to merge their businesses. Maybe something good will come of these events after all, if the rift between the two families can be healed."

She looked down, fingered the Bible, and then looked at Jono. "Kumar's sponsoring a school reunion. I think he hopes it will bury any lingering ghosts. Will you come?"

She was once again a vulnerable young woman. Her eyes pleaded with Jono.

"And spend time with you? I wouldn't miss it for the world."

CHAPTER SIXTY-FOUR

On Saturday morning, Rose drove herself and Dr Emma back to Ol Pejeta Conservancy to check the progress of Ringo, the orphan Rhino.

She drove the back, less-used route to the conservancy.

"What a state this road is," exclaimed Dr Emma. She was thrown sideways as the car lumbered over a deep furrow.

"They shouldn't let lorries down it in the wet season as they get stuck. Just look at the deep ruts that have baked hard in the sun."

Rose peered out of the windscreen and jerked the steering wheel to the right. "It's made worse when other vehicles attempt to pass the stationary lorries. This track has become wider and wider, it's a real mess. I keep hearing rumours it's going to be tarmacked, but nothing ever happens."

She turned off the road, and after completing the formalities at the Ol Pejeta entrance gate, they drove into the conservancy. The area along the track was wooded, with gaps between trees giving glimpses of the large plains beyond.

Rose spotted groups of animals grazing in the distance. As the bushes on the left thinned out, they spotted three rhino. She stopped the car so they could watch them.

"Oh look, they have a baby with them," cried Dr Emma. "I'm no good at telling the difference, are they black or white rhino? And don't tell me it's the colour, I know both species are steely grey." Dr Emma chuckled.

"My eyesight isn't great, but I think they're black, as they look smaller and more compact. Oh yes, look, that one's nibbling a bush. Black rhino have pitted lips, enabling them to bite leaves and twigs. They like browsing for their food. The flatter, broader lips of the white rhino makes it difficult for them to get hold of branches. Their mouths work more like a lawnmower along the grassy savannah."

They drove on and Rose parked once again by the caretakers' wooden hut. Zachariah met them, but his face was glum and he wrung his hands. "Little Ringo is no better. He spends most of the day lying down. He won't even talk to his big Uncle Sudan through the stall partition."

Dr Emma turned to Rose. "Can you take some blood? I've discussed the matter with the management team, and they've agreed that we can send blood to a lab in South Africa for testing."

Rose reached into the back of her Defender and removed her green veterinary bag. Once inside Ringo's stall, she unpacked needles, tubing, and vials in which to collect the blood. Ringo lifted his head as Rose ripped open the needle packet.

"Steady," said Zachariah. "He may not see very well, but his hearing is good and he didn't like that noise."

"Can you fetch a bucket of warm water, and a cloth or sponge?" she asked Zachariah. He left the enclosure as she continued her preparations. She handed the tube and vials to Dr Emma, as Zachariah returned with the bucket.

"OK, we need to be steady so as not to frighten him, but we must be decisive, as I suspect we only have one chance at this. Zachariah, as he knows you best, can you wet the inside of his front leg with your damp cloth? It'll help me to see the vein."

Zachariah did as instructed. Rose knelt beside him.

"It's OK, my friend." Zachariah spoke gently to the little Rhino.

Rose quickly stuck the needle up into the prominent leg vein, gave it a twist, and blood began to drip out.

"The tube, please," she requested from Dr Emma. Once the tube was attached to the needle, she attached a vial which began to fill with the young rhino's blood.

Zachariah stroked him and said, "My friend, be brave. These ladies are trying to help you."

She collected six samples in case any were damaged on their journey to South Africa. She removed the needle and watched Zachariah continue to stroke Ringo. She was worried. He'd hardly reacted when she inserted the needle.

"What is he eating?" she asked.

"Mostly milk formula," Zachariah replied. "We still prepare a small amount of his food, but he only nibbles at it."

Ringo laid his head back on the straw and closed his eyes.

Back at the car, Dr Emma addressed Zachariah. "We will let you know as soon as we have the results, but I'm afraid it doesn't look good." She reached out and touched Zachariah's arm. "I'm sorry. I know how fond of him you are, and all the hard work you and your team have put in, caring for him."

CHAPTER SIXTY-FIVE

T he next week passed uneventfully, for which Rose was grateful. She made a point of spending quality time with Craig each day. She invited three of his friends around for lunch on their patio on Wednesday and they visited another friend at his ranch in Laikipia on Friday.

On Sunday morning, Kipto was preparing Sunday lunch while Rose and Craig relaxed on the patio. Izzy, Rose's black and white cat, was curled up beside her.

Rose put her phone down, looked at Craig, and said, "Chloe's just sent me a message. She says Dan wants to go to Cape Chestnut for curry lunch with a group from the British Army. So she won't be joining us."

Craig was reading the Sunday Telegraph newspaper, from the UK, on Rose's tablet. She had persuaded him to subscribe so that he didn't spend all his time trying to complete crosswords, and asking her to help to fill in the squares. The Telegraph had a daily crossword and whilst he couldn't write the answers on the screen, he could still work out the solutions.

He looked up, "That doesn't sound like Chloe's cup of

tea. I thought she'd rather come here with Thabiti and Marina."

Rose stretched her arms. "I'm sure she would, but I think she's trying to accommodate Dan a little more, and do the things he wants to when he's home. You know how worried I've been about her relationship. Hopefully this is a move in the right direction."

Potto, Rose's terrier, wandered out of the house and leapt onto Craig's lap.

Craig stroked Potto and asked, "Did you tell me Pearl is coming? Does that mean she's getting better?"

Rose tilted her head and answered, "I'm not sure, but I know Thabiti wants her to become more independent, so they can both move forward with their lives."

Rose, Craig, Marina, Thabiti, and Pearl were all seated around the outdoor dining table. Thabiti's fluffy white dog, Pixel, was attempting to jump onto Craig's vacated patio chair, but Potto, who was already curled up on the cushions, was giving it no room. After several futile attempts, Pixel padded into the house.

"Shoo," called Kipto as she emerged from the house. She removed a hand from the wooden board she carried and waved it at Pixel.

"Do you not feed this dog?" She looked at Thabiti with wide, accusing eyes.

Thabiti glanced at her and quickly looked down, grinning.

She placed the board, on which were two roast chickens, in front of Craig.

Craig leaned across to Thabiti. "Can you help me carve?"

Thabiti leaned back and placed his hands on the table. "But I've no idea how to."

"That's OK, I'll tell you what to do. It's just that I can't keep the birds still with my left hand whilst I carve with my right."

Thabiti reluctantly pushed back his chair and stood on Craig's left side.

Rose turned to Pearl and placed a hand on her arm. "You're looking well. There's a glint in your eyes I haven't seen before, and you've had your hair done."

Marina exclaimed. "I love the burgundy colour. And you're really brave having it cut so short. Is it a pixie style?"

Pearl glanced at Marina and then Rose. She gulped, held her head up, and said, "Thank you for inviting me to lunch. It's the first time I've been out, apart from my visits to the hospital and of course, this week, to the salon." She patted her hair with a manicured hand. Her nails were short and painted the same colour as her hair.

She continued, "It's time for me to rejoin the real world, and getting my hair done is the first step. Do you like it? I wanted something easy to care for but different, and not the long braids I used to wear."

Marina looked at Pearl in admiration and said, "I wish I was brave enough to try something new. My hair has always been long and straight and I've never really thought about changing it."

Pearl placed her hands on the table. "If you'd like, I could go with you to the salon next week. You could treat yourself to a manicure and pedicure and we could look at hair designs together."

Marina's eyes shone. "Wow, I've never had anyone to do that with before. Yes, please," she nodded enthusiastically.

Rose watched Craig instructing Thabiti at the far end of the table. His hand was placed over Thabiti's as he guided the knife. "There, cut down steadily, but with enough force to slice through the breast meat. Well done. Now move the knife across one slice width and cut. It's just a matter of repeating the slicing until you reach the breast bone."

Kipto placed bowls of boiled carrots and cabbage on the table.

Rose turned to Marina. "How is your family? I hadn't expected to see you again so soon."

Marina tapped the table. "I think they're trying to put the Rhino Charge events behind them. There was a big meeting this week with Gautam and Kumar Chauhan about merging the businesses, but I'm not sure of the outcome."

Marina and Rose looked across at Thabiti as Craig explained, "Now we cut here to remove the leg."

Marina twiddled her fingers and said, "Thabiti gave me an open invite to stay at Guinea Fowl Cottage." She looked across at Pearl. "I hope that's all right with you."

Pearl shrugged. "No problem. It's nice to have some female company."

Marina extended her arm. "I'll spend next week here, sorting out deliveries and finding somewhere to store items, particularly chilled and frozen foods, before we can collect them for the lodge. Companies deliver on different days, and I can't come into Nanyuki, or send a vehicle every day. It's just not economical."

Kipto placed delicious-smelling roast potatoes and Yorkshire puddings on the table.

"And then I'm going to the lodge so I can work out if we need any more staff. And also get to know the area, and the best places for bush walks and game drives." Marina turned to Rose and cocked her head to one side. "Someone told me there are canopy walks and blue pools in the Ngare Ndare forest. Do you know them?"

Rose nodded. "They're lovely and you can swim in the pools. Watch out for elephants, though. Sometimes they walk right under the rope bridges."

Pearl opened her mouth, hesitated, and then asked, "That sounds fun. Could I come with you?"

"Of course, and we can take a picnic. What do you think, Mama Rose? Do you want to come as well?"

Rose placed her hand over Marina's. "Thank you, but I think you young people should go together. And if Dan's gone back to work, why not ask Chloe to join you? Make it a girl's trip."

Thabiti looked up and smiled proudly, "All done. Shall I serve out?"

He divided the carved meat onto plates and they helped each other to potatoes, vegetables, and Yorkshire puddings. Kipto placed a jug of gravy on the table.

Rose bent her head, murmured a short prayer, and said, "Please start."

Thabiti tucked in with gusto while Pearl took small, dainty bites.

Craig looked around the table and smiled, a look of satisfaction on his face. "So you three are going to a brand new lodge in Borana for a month?"

Marina and Thabiti locked eyes.

Thabiti said, "Yes. It should be fun. I've been learning all about the cutting edge solar system they've installed for lighting, and they're also considering growing food for the lodge with a hydroponic system, as it needs less water."

Rose asked, "When do the family arrive?"

Marina answered. "The first week of June. They're coming over to run in the Lewa Marathon."

Thabiti swallowed a mouthful and said, "Like Chloe. I bumped into her when she was out on a run this week. She said the break over the Rhino Charge has helped and she feels fresher now. I might go with her on my bike next week and find some tracks to run and ride on up Mount Kenya. She said she needs a bit more hill work."

Craig addressed Rose. "You need to decide if you're helping with the water stop this year. Bruce wants to know so he can organise tickets."

She answered, "I'm not sure I want to, not without you. I thought that perhaps, after the marathon, we could find somewhere to stay for a night or two and rediscover Lewa and Borana."

Marina bobbed up and down excitedly. "Why don't I see if you can stay in one of the guest cottages? The family are leaving soon after the marathon, and there are no more guests scheduled whilst we're there."

Rose turned to Marina. "That's very kind, but I don't think your family will want just anyone staying."

"You're not anyone. I'll ask Ollie, and he can always say no. How exciting if we're all in Borana."

Craig looked across at Pearl. "Are you going as well?"

Her head bowed, she looked over at Craig and replied, "Yes, I'm doing a yoga course while I'm there." She raised her head. "I started classes at the Cottage Hospital, and to my surprise I enjoyed them. Also, it'll keep me out of Marina and Thabiti's way when the family are staying. It's the same weekend as the Lewa marathon."

Rose sat back. "I have a good feeling about this. It would be great if we could all spend some time in Borana." She looked directly at Craig. "And maybe you and I could drive over and watch the marathon and support Chloe. It would mean an early start, but what do you think?"

"If you don't mind driving, that would be splendid."

Thabiti pushed his empty plate to one side. "I think it would be a great idea. Especially as Craig can make sure you keep out of trouble. Not that I can see anyone being murdered at the marathon."

Rose answered, "Let's hope not. But you never know, human nature being what it is."

Dear Reader

I do hope you've enjoyed Rhino Charge. If you enjoyed the book, please leave a review on the platform you bought from, and any others you are willing and able to post on. Reviews will help bring Rhino Charge to the attention of other readers. A couple of lines highlighting what you like most, such as characters, setting, plot etc. are sufficient.

I wrote an epilogue about Lavanya, and what happens to her, as soon as I finished the main book. If you would like a copy please visit https://dl.bookfunnel.com/wmoyd0pvyt or email me at victoria@victoriatait.com and I will send you a link.

When you request the epilogue you will sign up to my book club, where you will hear from me about my books, author life, new releases and special offers. I don't send spam and you can unsubscribe at any time.

I wrote the book in 2020 and often found it hard to concentrate, or settle down to write, with the difficulties and issues we all faced. But transporting myself to Kenya, and transferring words from head onto paper, were a huge release from the real world.

I didn't have the opportunity to visit or take part in the Rhino Charge, but I knew many competitors, officials and organisers. It continues to be an exciting event which raises huge amounts of money to protect and preserve wildlife and forest habitats.

It was fascinating learning more about the history of the Indian population in Kenya. I knew many when I lived there and their culture has had a lasting impact, particularly on the Kenyan cuisine. On the 22nd July 2017 President Uhuru Kenyatta officially recognised the Indian community as the forty-fourth tribe in Kenya.

I did meet Ringo, the orphan southern white rhino calf, and was saddened by his death in July 2016. Ol Pejeta Conservancy said that "during his short life, Ringo inspired hundreds of people worldwide with his playful antics and irresistible charm. In simply being himself, he helped raise awareness about the plight of rhino in Africa."

I particularly enjoyed writing the multiple character scenes and watching Marina, Thabiti, and Chloe grow as they interacted with each other and with 'Mama Rose'. I hope you'll join them in the next book, Jackal and Hide, where Marina and Thabiti begin to find their calling in life. But there is trouble for Chloe, heartache for Rose, and of course, another murder to be solved.

Best wishes

Victoria

To Download the the Epilogue visit
https://dl.bookfunnel.com/7c57s5wtt6

ABOUT THE AUTHOR

Victoria Tait is the author of the enchanting Kenya Kanga Mystery series. She's drawn on her 8 years experience living in rural Kenya, with her family, to write vivid and evocative descriptions. Her readers feel the heat, taste the dryness and smell the dust of Africa. Her elderly amateur sleuth, "Mama Rose" Hardie is Agatha Christie's Miss Marple reincarnated and living in Kenya.

Like all good military wives, Victoria follows the beat of the drum and has recently moved to war scarred Sarajevo in Bosnia. She has two fast growing teenage boys. She enjoys horse riding and mountain biking. Victoria is looking forward to the sun, sand and seafood of neighbouring Croatia when the world returns to normal.

You can find Victoria at VictoriaTait.com or at Goodreads and BookBub.

If you would like to email Victoria her address is victoria@victoriatait.com

A Kanga Press Ebook

First published in 2021 by Kanga Press

Ebook first published in 2021 by Kanga Press Copyright Victoria Tait 2021

Book Cover Design by ebooklaunch.com

Editing Cassandra Dunn and Allie Douglas

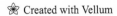 Created with Vellum

Made in the USA
Columbia, SC
07 February 2021

32502192R00164